TREASURE
— OF THE —
BATTERSEA
BLUFFS

Barbara —
So enjoyed
meeting you!

God Bless,
Sarah

Sarah Norkus

Treasure
— of the —
Battersea
Bluffs

TATE PUBLISHING
AND ENTERPRISES, LLC

Published by Tate Publishing & Enterprises, LLC
127 E. Trade Center Terrace | Mustang, Oklahoma 73064 USA
1.888.361.9473 | www.tatepublishing.com

Tate Publishing is committed to excellence in the publishing industry. The company reflects the philosophy established by the founders, based on Psalm 68:11,
"The Lord gave the word and great was the company of those who published it."

Book design copyright © 2015 by Tate Publishing, LLC. All rights reserved.
Cover design by Nikolai Purpura
Interior design by Jomar Ouano

Published in the United States of America

ISBN: 978-1-63449-191-4
1. Fiction / Action & Adventure
2. Fiction / Historical
14.11.12

To all those readers, like me,
who love a good adventure story.

ACKNOWLEDGMENTS

I have a heart full of gratitude for everyone who helped me on my journey to turn a germ of an idea into a story to entertain the minds of the young and old.

Thank you, Dr. Bonnie Harvey, my agent, editor, and friend, for your unwavering faith in my writing ability.

Tate Publishing Company and their hard-working production crew have turned my labor of love into a work of art.

The many historians I consulted gave me invaluable information on the customs and everyday life of the colonists before the American Revolution. And most importantly, they corrected me when I got it wrong. (No, it's not a privy, it's a necessary house.)

My family and friends spent hours reading and critiquing the manuscript. Love you all.

And may I end with a very simple thank you to my readers, for whom I write.

Thank you, and may God bless you abundantly.

CHAPTER 1

APRIL 2009

The bumblebee made lazy circles in the air as it skimmed past the large white oak and flew toward the blossoms of the dogwood tree. Flitting from flower to flower, the bee sucked up nectar with the feathery tip of her tongue. The pollen clung to her legs as she lifted off a blossom and skirted the old man laboriously shuffling his way around the circular dirt drive. The bee's new goal was a large brown object three yards past the elderly man.

Unaware that she was the bee's target, the chestnut mare blew air out of her nostrils and pawed the ground. She swished her tail as a strong breeze sent errant dogwood blossoms onto her back and rump. The tall young man in the powdered wig leaned forward in the saddle and patted her neck fondly as he waited for the wreath-laying ceremony to begin on this fine April morning at Battersea.

The bee settled on a blossom resting directly behind the saddle, causing the mare to flick her tail in annoyance. The bumblebee, provoked, plunged her stinger into the chestnut's rump. Eyes wide with pain, the mare reared, unseating her rider into the shrubs beside the porch steps. The horse bolted up the concrete steps directly in front of her, hooves stomping over the front door threshold of the two-hundred-and-thirty-year-old Palladian villa. Her eyes reflected her terror as she avoided the hand that tried to grab her halter. She turned right, galloping through the bare rooms of the east wing. As a wall loomed up in front of her, the mare reared then plunged her hooves into the old floorboards. There was a snap and a crack appeared. The mare reared and plunged again. A small piece of the wooden plank broke off and disappeared beneath the floor.

Em and Josh stood stunned next to the display table as three men tried to wrestle the panicked animal out of the room. Curiosity overcame shock as Em walked over to the damaged floor. She dropped to her knees and grasped the edge of floorboard to look into the cavity opened by the horse's hooves. Her eyes widened. There was something beneath the ancient floor planks. She reached into hole and her hand came into contact with something long and hard like a pencil. She pulled it closer to her face and froze in shock. Horrified, she gazed at the small, delicate finger bones of a skeleton as a vision filled her mind.

The young girl was dressed in colonial period garb, similar to the costume Em wore. Her brown cap became eschewed on her white-blonde hair as she struggled with a man twice her height. Above a smattering of freckles her blue eyes were wide with terror. Her bloodless lips trembled. Em's view only afforded her a glimpse of the man's back as he reached for the hem of the girl's dress. The girl sucked in a breath for a bloodcurdling scream, but the man's hand covered her mouth, choking it off. Even in her terror she had the presence of mind to clamp her strong teeth on the hand that covered her mouth. The man jerked his hand back in pain, but only for a second. Raising it high, he brought it back down in a hard slap across the girl's cheek. The blow knocked her to the floor. A sickening thud followed as the girl's head hit a stack of bricks.

The man knelt by the girl's side. Em watched as he slapped her on each cheek hard, causing her head to flop back and forth. When she didn't respond, he glanced over at the doorway to the next room. Em saw his worried profile. Tipping his tricorn hat up, he wiped sweat from his brow as he looked around the room. His gaze lingered on a large hollow space in the corner of the room where wooden planks had yet to be laid to complete the floor of the room. The assailant dragged the girl's body by the arm over to the cavity. He rolled her onto the dirt between the two exposed joists shoving her body beneath the wide wooden planks. Grunting and sweating, he continued to push until she was well hidden. He rose to his feet and quickly exited through a rear door.

Stunned and shaking violently, Em said, "No, no, no, please, God, don't let this be true," as the vision faded then disappeared. She wrenched her fingers away from the gap and jumped to her feet as vertigo hit her with a vengeance. Groping blindly with one hand and covering her mouth with the other as the nausea hit, Em turned and stumbled forward. As all feeling left her legs and she started to collapse to the floor, Em had one coherent thought, *Oh, no, please. Not again.*

Josh had not noticed Em walking toward the gap in the floor made by the mare. His eyes had been riveted on the three men trying to wrestle the panicked horse out of the villa. Once they managed to get her out the front door and onto the porch, Josh moved to the nearby window and watched through the pane of glass as they led her down the steps of the front porch, her flanks still quivering with fear. One of the men, wearing a ponytailed wig and tricorn hat, was whispering in her ear and softly rubbing her velvet nose. Within a few moments, the mare calmed down, dropping her head and lightly bumping the man's arm. The man gently pulled on the bridle leading the mare around the dirt drive in front of the villa.

Turning away from the window, Josh heard Em say something about God. She was white as a ghost and stumbling toward him. Rushing to her, Josh caught her in his arms just as her knees started to buckle. Josh staggered as a feeling of dizziness swept over him. Shaking his head, he tried to dispatch the wooziness. The vertigo was getting worse and he felt as if he would vomit. Josh tamped down on his gag reflex, shut his eyes and dropped to the floor on his rear end, holding on tight to Em. His mind became a dark void as he passed out, tipping to the right onto his side, Em still cradled in his arms.

CHAPTER 2

E m blinked her eyes open. She lay on her side on a wooden floor. She breathed in and immediately sneezed as sawdust entered her nose. Putting a hand to the floor, she tried to push up to a seated position but was stopped by something tugging at her waist. Em's eyes widened with fear at the hand gripping her dove-gray dress. She yanked her dress away from the hand, and digging her black half boots into the floor, she pushed backward. The rest of the body attached to the hand came into view. It was Josh. Reversing direction, she crawled over to her boyfriend.

"Josh!" Em shook one shoulder. "Josh, it's me, Em. Can you hear me?"

When Josh was still unresponsive after a couple of minutes, Em started yelling for help. She paused to listen for the sound of running feet, but there were none. Where was everyone? Why didn't they answer? Em climbed to her feet and staggered as a feeling of lightheadedness hit her. A bit unsteady she walked over to the window and stopped dead. The glass panes were gone. It was just a wooden frame. Purposely ignoring what her brain was trying to tell her, Em leaned out the window. Gone, everyone was gone. And the landscape was different. The circular drive was gone. A rutted track made by heavy wheels led straight from the front of the house to a dirt road in the distance. There was no stucco covering the red brick of the outside walls. The porch was gone. Correction, it had not been built *yet*. There was no use denying the obvious. She was in the past—*again*. Turning back into the room, she noticed that the display table was gone and a small portion of the floor had not been laid. Em frowned. There was something familiar about that cavity in the floor. She glanced at Josh passed out on the floor and two thoughts collided in her mind. *Oh no, Josh had gone back with her! The body of the young girl was hidden in that hole!*

Em's body shook as the enormity of the situation hit her. She walked over to the area of unfinished floor and dropped down on a trembling knee. She held her breath as she bent down and looked under the laid boards. The air in her lungs whooshed out in relief as she realized the young girl's body was not there. Turning her head, she looked at her boyfriend curled up as if in a peaceful slumber. She had never told Josh about the one other time she went back in time. *Well, they do say confession is good for the soul. I guess today would be an excellent time to start.* She glanced down again at the large space where the floorboards needed to be laid. *And what about the girl in her vision?* Em's gaze moved back to Josh. He was the more immediate problem. Trying to still her trembling, Em approached Josh. She lifted the hem of her dress and dropped to her knees. Em smoothed back his blond bangs and prayed that he would not be very angry with her.

Just as her knees were beginning to protest the pressure of the hardwood floor, Josh began to stir. Opening his eyes, he stared up at Em. He placed the palm of his right hand on the floor and tried to sit up. Em grabbed his right arm and helped him to a seated position.

Josh lifted both hands to his head and groaned.

Em said, "Are you okay, Josh? The wooziness should pass in a couple of minutes."

His memory returning, Josh reached out and grabbed Em's shoulders. "Are you all right? You collapsed and I had to catch you."

"I'm fine, I just passed out. So did you. How do you feel?"

Josh moved his head to the right and then to the left. "Okay, the dizziness has passed."

Josh uncrossed his legs and then pushed to his feet with Em's help. "What happened to us? That was so weird, both of us passing out at the same time. Maybe there was something in the lemonade we drank."

"That wouldn't be my first guess," Em mumbled to herself.

"What did you say?"

"Nothing. Look, Josh, I have something I have to…"

"Where's the display table? Why have some of the planks been removed from the floor?" Josh said as he gazed around the room.

Nervously rubbing her hands together, Em began, "Well, you see…"

Josh's eyes widened as he stared at the window with no glass in it. "Who broke the window? How long have we been out anyway?"

Josh glanced at the leather banded watch on his left wrist and gasped in amazement. "Thirty minutes! We were unconscious for half an hour and no one checked on us? They removed the display table, pulled up planks, broke the window, and just walked around us on the floor!"

Shocked and bewildered, Josh looked at Em, who was uncharacteristically silent.

"Why aren't you upset? We could have been lying here dying for all anyone knew! I didn't want to dress up in this ridiculous costume and come here to begin with. Now I have a headache and you had better believe it's time to leave." Josh glanced out the glassless window. "Where is everyone?"

Just as Em was about to explain their situation, a sound caught her attention. She looked through the window as three men on horseback turned down the rutted road toward the villa, two gentlemen by the look of their dress and a black man, probably a slave. She sucked in her breath. If she could see them, they could see her and Josh. Grabbing the sleeve of his white blouse, she yanked as hard as she could, knocking Josh onto his butt.

"Why did you jerk me off my feet!" His face was turning red. "I was about to get those riders' attention and find out what the heck is going on!"

"Listen, I know what's going on. But right now we have to stay hidden." Her green eyes bored into Josh's blue ones. "Please, you have to trust me. Those men cannot know we're here."

"Em…"

"Shush, they're getting close enough to hear."

Em scooted close to the window frame and peeked cautiously around the corner. The three men had dismounted and were tying the reins of the horses to a hitching post. The man closest to her was tall with a tricorn hat atop brown hair tied back with a brown ribbon. His solid frame was encased in buff-colored breeches with a matching waistcoat. His attire was similar to the costumed men she had seen around the estate an hour ago.

When he turned his face in her direction, Em whispered in shock, "It's Colonel John Banister!"

His round, florid face matched exactly the drawing in the brochure that they had been handing out all morning. He was the original owner of the villa and a revolutionary war hero. The Battersea Foundation, named for the villa, was trying to restore the house to its original magnificence with the help of donations through fund-raising events.

"Hey, where are those little canvas tents that were all over the place?" Josh whispered back.

Em ignored Josh as she stared at the profile of the man next to the colonel. When he turned in her direction, Em felt her body go rigid with fear. It was the man from her vision. Shorter and leaner than his companion, he was dressed all in black except for white hose. His sleek black hair was also pulled back beneath his tricorn and tied with a piece of leather.

Breathing quietly, Josh had moved directly behind Em, peering over the top of her head. Questions darted back and forth in his mind, but he pressed his lips together tight, not blurting one out. He studied the men. They were in period costume. The lone black man looked young, maybe sixteen, the same age as Josh and Em. He was probably playing the role of slave to one of the other men. The taller of the two white men requested something of the young black man, and he strode away to do his bidding. The shorter man addressed his companion, and leaning into the window, Josh could hear what they were saying.

<hr />

"Banister, this is a fine piece of architecture. I am most grateful for the invitation to examine the workmanship."

Angus Blackburn's gaze encompassed the five-part brick structure. The center of the structure was two stories. Each wing had two large rooms, one with no second floor and the other with a second-floor attic.

"When you expressed your interest in Andrea Palladio style villas at the meeting of the Burgesses in Williamsburg, I was delighted to accommodate you, sir."

"That was quite an address by the governor, Lord Botetourte, yesterday," Blackburn said as they climbed the front steps.

"He is King George's puppet. I dismissed his words immediately," John Banister replied flatly as he stepped over the threshold into the entryway.

Blackburn paused to examine the Chinese lattice work stair railing that led to the upper floor. His gaze turned to the left at the sound of hammering in the west wing. "I concur. The parliament's taxes diminish the goodly profits from my tobacco. King George is sitting on a powder keg. The protests and violence will only continue to escalate."

Banister bowed slightly and indicated the main room with his right hand. "This, sir, is the salon."

Striding forward, Blackburn glanced at the pane-less windows. "When do you expect to finish?"

"About six months to completion."

Both men paused in their conversation as footsteps echoed in the next room.

"Ah, Mister Fletcher, may I introduce Mister Angus Blackburn."

Fletcher bowed with deference to Blackburn. "Your servant, sir."

Banister continued, "Fletcher is my overseer, and this is his indentured servant, Martha."

Blackburn's eyes widened in shock. She was the most beautiful girl he had ever seen. She was very petite, no more than fifteen years old, with long white-blonde hair and cornflower-blue eyes.

Unnerved by the intensity of the gentleman's stare, Martha quickly curtsied. His dark eyes never left her face as her master discussed business with Banister.

Remembering a task that needed finishing, Mister Fletcher's gaze turned to Martha. "Lass, fetch a broom and sweep up the wood leavings and sawdust in the east wing."

Martha dashed off to do her master's bidding as Mister Fletcher turned to his employer. "The additional floorboards were delivered early this morn, so the laborers will finish the floors in both wings before dusk."

"And what of the progress on the digging of the well?"

"Progress has come to a halt, sir. We have encountered bedrock. We will be moving to a location a bit south of the present one."

"Please accompany me, Mister Fletcher, I wish to view the new location."

Banister turned to Blackburn. "I do beg your pardon, Blackburn. I shall be but a moment, sir."

"Please, Banister, take all the time that you require. By your leave, I will study the molding in these two rooms to my right."

"You have my permission, sir."

Em and Josh had pressed their backs against the east wing wall when the men entered the building so they would go unnoticed. The empty rooms had amplified the men's conversation, and Em's heart filled with dread. Martha must be the young girl in the vision, and Blackburn, her murderer. Quickly, she looked around the empty room for a hiding place. If her vision was correct, Blackburn and the girl would come together in this room. Turning her head to the right, she looked at Josh as she raised her right finger and pointed to a framed doorway that led to a small east wing porch. She slid her body sideways along the wall as Josh got her meaning and slid ahead of her. Arriving at the doorway, Josh slid around the corner and took two steps to the edge of the porch. Em followed suit, clearing the doorway and pressing close to Josh.

Josh's breath was warm as he whispered in her ear, "Is this some kind of reenactment we're playing a role in?"

Before Em could answer, they both heard boot heels sound on the steps at the front of the house. They peered around the corner of the building just as Banister and a gaunt older man strode toward the west side of the house, deep in conversation.

Josh whispered again in Em's ear, "Wasn't there a wide porch at the front of the house?"

Em froze at the sound of loud footsteps coming into the room they had just vacated. A male voice muttered nervously, "Hurry, lass, time is escaping." Barely discernible footsteps drew closer to the room.

"Ah, there you are, Martha."

Em dared a peek around the doorframe. Blackburn's back was to her. Martha was staring at him with a straw broom in one hand and uncertainty written on her face.

"You wished something of me, sir?"

Em's heart started to pound in her chest, and instinctively she grabbed Josh's arm in a tight grip. Josh peered over Em's shoulder to get a glimpse of the actors in the room. Em had not answered his question, but he was sure this must be a dress rehearsal for a play.

His heart full of greedy lust for the beautiful young girl, Blackburn asked, "Martha, how much time will Mister Fletcher require of Mister Banister?"

In a small voice, Martha said, "I do not know, sir. I will hasten to my master and inquire."

As she turned to go, Blackburn grabbed her arm, causing the broom to fall to the floor. Not for the first time, insurmountable desire had chased away all moral decency.

"You mistake my intentions. I do not wish you to disturb your master. I merely did not want an interruption at an inappropriate time."

Martha tried to remove her arm from Blackburn's tight grip. "Please, sir, I do not take your meaning."

"I mean to have you, now, and quickly before your master and Banister return. There is no need to fight me. In five minutes you will be at your task, sweeping the floor for your master."

Josh nearly made Em jump out of her skin when he whispered, "This seems so real. They're great actors. But I don't like the scene they are acting out."

Em ignored Josh as she watched Martha struggling with Blackburn in earnest. Fear filled her blue eyes as she beseeched Blackburn, "Please, sir, I beg of you to release me."

Em took a deep breath and prayed for God to be with her as she stepped over the threshold and into the room. Confused, Josh stepped through the door behind her.

"Let her go," Em said, with a slight quaver to her words.

Blackburn wheeled around, his grip still tight on Martha's arm. Martha stopped struggling, and relief filled her lovely adolescent face.

Blackburn glared at the young woman who spoke like a foreigner. "'Tis none of your concern, lass. Leave at once."

Josh looked at Em's face. She was not acting. She was terrified. Something was seriously wrong here.

"Hey, man, let go of that girl," Josh said as he put a bolstering arm around Em.

Blackburn looked with disdain at the young man dressed as a common laborer. He ignored his abuse of the queen's English.

"How dare you address me thus? What is your purpose here?"

Before Josh could speak, Em interrupted, "We are seeking positions with Colonel, ah, I mean, Mister Banister."

Josh glanced at Em, perplexed at her words.

Martha again tried to pull away as Blackburn replied, "The gentleman is with the overseer. Now leave."

Furious at Blackburn's treatment of the girl, Josh strode across the room and jerked Blackburn's hand off Martha. "I said, let her go!"

As Blackburn stiffened in disbelief, Martha took two steps, swayed on her feet, and collapsed to the floor.

"She's fainted!" Em exclaimed.

Josh started to bend toward Martha's crumpled form as Blackburn pulled a knife out of his boot and brandished it at

Josh, nicking his wrist. Josh stared in disbelief as a small pool of blood formed.

"I shall see you hang for this insult." Blackburn's face had turned a vivid red.

Rage and confusion crossed Josh's features. "Did you say hang? You just cut me with a knife! You have a serious screw loose, dude. The police can deal with you."

As Josh reached into his pocket for his cell phone, Blackburn lunged across the room and grabbed Em's arm with one hand as he pressed the blade of the knife against her side with the other.

"Remove your weapon and drop it to the floor."

In an instant, rage was replaced by shock and fear. "Hey, okay, just a cell phone." Josh placed his phone slowly on the floor.

Blackburn stared in confusion at the small rectangular object and back at Josh. "'Tis trickery. Remove your weapon."

Josh patted down his pockets. "Look, man, I don't have a weapon. Please just let her go and we'll leave. I swear."

"You shall leave," Blackburn stated with satisfaction, "with your hands bound behind you and seated in a wagon removing you to the Williamsburg's gaol."

Em stood completely still, afraid to move a muscle. She could feel the sharp tip of the blade poking through the fabric of her dress. It brought to mind another time when she had been in a similar position. She had gone back in time to 1865, and an enraged prison guard had tried to attack her. She had shot him with a rifle. Shaking the thought away, Em tried desperately to figure out a way to stop Blackburn from harming herself or Josh.

Two seconds later, coming up with a solution to their dilemma became a moot point because Josh had launched himself at Blackburn. He barreled into him as if he were taking out an offensive lineman on the football field. Em's arm was jerked loose, and she fled to the corner by the door. Josh was quick to gain his feet, very much aware of the knife inches

from his abdomen. Blackburn was just as quick, leaping upright and brandishing the knife in a wide arc. Both men crouched, looking for an opening. Em decided despite her misgivings to the contrary she would have to involve John Banister.

"Josh, I'm going to get Mr. Banister."

Quicker than she would have thought possible, Blackburn was back at her side, the blade against her throat before she could take her first step.

"No, lass, you will not spin a web of lies to that fine gentleman. I will tell the tale when he returns."

Blackburn stared hard at Josh. "Now slowly, lad, you will retreat to the far corner, sit, and put your hands atop your head or I will slit her throat."

Having no other choice, Josh did as he was told, praying desperately that the actor's mind was not so far gone that he would murder Em. His fear was so great he began to shake with it.

CHAPTER 3

APRIL 1770

E zra swung the axe high over his head and paused for two seconds before bringing it down in a swift arc, burying the head in the trunk of the pine tree for the last time. He watched as the small tree fell with a muffled crash on top of the soft carpet of rotting leaves and vegetation from the spring rains. Still gripping the handle of the axe with one hand, he slipped the other into the pocket of his faded brown breeches for the scrap of muslin to wipe sweat from his nut-brown face. The breeze coming off the river was a blessing, but the sweat still poured off him from his exertion. He paused in the act of wiping the lower half of his face. He was facing one of the back windows of the last room of the east wing. A white man had just thrown himself at Master Blackburn and knocked him to the floor.

Ezra shoved the muslin back into his pocket and rushed to the pane-less window in time to see the two men in crouched positions facing each other. He had turned slightly to run and find Master Banister when he noticed Martha crumpled upon the floor of the room. *Who would attack her thus?*

He looked up as another young girl said, in oddly accented English, that she would go for Master Banister. Blackburn swiveled, rushed to the girl, and grabbed her as he brought a knife to her throat. Without conscious thought, Ezra sped around the corner of the house and up the few steps to the back door of the room in time to hear Blackburn order the man to sit in the corner. As Blackburn started to turn at the sound of footsteps behind him, Ezra only had a few seconds to access the situation as his grip tightened on the axe handle.

Believing Martha to be dead and the other young girl about to suffer the same fate, he slowly raised the axe and brought the blunt end down on the tricorn hat covering the crown of Blackburn's head. Blackburn dropped like a rock, pricking Em's neck with the knife blade in the process. Em brought her fingers up to the left side of her neck. They came away smeared with blood. Josh jumped up and rushed to Em, reaching into the pocket of his gray knee breeches for the linen handkerchief that was part of the colonial garb he was wearing.

Pressing it against the wound, he said, "It's nothing, Em, really, just a scratch."

Em's eyes traveled down to the man on the floor and then back up to the black teenager who had saved them.

"Thank you, you saved our lives." Em tried to control the quaver in her voice. "My name is Em...ah, Emily and this is Joshua."

"They call me Ezra, miss. But there is no need to thank me."

Ezra glanced down at Blackburn then back up at the teens. "We must flee or the three of us will hang. Master Blackburn is one of the most important and influential men of these colonies. When he regains consciousness, his tale will be believed, ours will not."

Ezra's gaze turned to Martha. They would be blamed for her demise also. Master Banister was kind and reasonable, but it would not matter. Even being white would not help the young miss and master. Suddenly aware of time escaping on invisible wings and the imminent arrival of his master, Ezra pointed through the back door and the woods to the left.

"Please, young master and miss, we must make haste into the woods!"

Josh removed his hand as Em grasped the hankie. "Hang? You're starting to sound as crazy as Blackburn. And why are you talking like a slave? This dress rehearsal, or whatever, is over."

Josh pointed to Blackburn lying at his feet. "This actor is a mental case. I'm calling the cops and having him arrested." Josh walked over to his cell phone and picked it up off the floor.

"Uh, Josh, I don't think you're going to get a signal," Em said.

"Sure I will. I called my mom earlier from this room." As Josh moved the cell phone around looking for a signal, voices could be heard coming from the west end of the building.

Ezra put aside his sudden curiosity about the strange contraption in Josh's hand and said, "We must make haste, now!"

Ezra bolted from the room, making a beeline for the cover of the woods. Em followed as fast as her legs would carry her, her fingers still pressing the handkerchief to her wound.

Josh said "Hey!" and chased after them.

Ezra entered the safety of the trees and wild undergrowth at the edge of the property and waited for Em and Josh to catch up. As soon as they did, he pushed through the underbrush of ferns, yellow forsythia, and multiple vines, moving deeper into the woods that followed the river. Once he was free of the underbrush, he continued on, ignoring Josh's demands to stop. His worn leather shoes trod upon the dead leaves, moss, and pine needles of the previous autumn. Hearing a commotion behind him, he halted and looked back. Josh had a hold of Em's arm and was pleading with her to go back to the house. Em removed the blood-streaked hankie from her neck and glared at Josh.

"Em, why are we running away like criminals? We didn't do anything wrong. I need to get back to my dad's car and call the police."

Taking out her fear on Josh, she blurted the truth and instantly regretted it. "There is no car and there are no police. They don't exist now!"

"What?" Josh simply stared at Em as he snapped his cell phone close and absentmindedly slipped it into the small pocket in his vest.

Stray strands of auburn hair had escaped from beneath Em's bun, and she impatiently brushed them from her face as she took a breath and tried to control her fear.

"Josh, I don't have time to explain this properly. I know you're going to think I'm crazy, but we are no longer in the twenty-first century. I'm guessing it must be the eighteenth century." Em quickly looked at Ezra. Now he would think she was delusional, too. But he wasn't paying attention. He was stashing the axe behind some bushes.

"Josh, we have to keep moving, I will explain as we follow Ezra." The wound felt clotted beneath her fingers, so Em shoved the handkerchief in the pocket of her dress.

Ezra started forward again at a fast pace. Josh followed lost in thought. *Why did Em say they were no longer in the twenty-first century? Even his girlfriend was delusional. He had heard of mass hysteria. Was there such a thing as mass hallucinations? Was he the only sane person in the area?* He shivered at the thought.

"...back in time before. It happened last summer."

"What? Start again, I missed it."

"Lower, your voice, I don't want Ezra to think we're crazy. I said I went back in time before, last summer."

Josh put a comforting arm around Em as they skirted a large elm tree. "Em, I think you're experiencing some kind of hallucination along with Ezra, who thinks he's a slave, and

Blackburn who thinks…well, it doesn't matter what he thinks, he's just plain crazy and needs to be locked up."

Em pulled away from Josh's arm in exasperation. "Josh, I am not hallucinating. Do you remember last summer when they did that write-up about me in the newspaper?"

"Sure, the article about you discovering the gold coins in a secret hiding place in the attic of that old house in Petersburg."

"One of the coins wasn't in the hole in the attic. It came back with me from the year 1865." Em sighed. "See, it all started when I found an old diary in the attic. I hid it in my capris, took it home, and read it. Well, I was upset because at the end of the diary Sarah's husband, Robert, was murdered and…"

"Who?"

"Sarah…she wrote the diary. The last entry talked about her confederate officer husband being murdered in a Union prison. Anyway, the day I went back into the past, I was upset. I had gone with my mom to the old Petersburg house, where I found the diary, to help her clean…and I started complaining to God about how unfair it was that Robert was murdered and my Aunt Katy was going to lose her house and I got cancer, and my dog dying…well, actually, I was doing more than complaining, I told God I didn't think he existed, and oh, boy did he prove me wrong.

"In the blink of an eye, God sent me back to the year 1865, and I had the opportunity to change what had happened to Robert. It's a long story, but you see, I did save Robert, and Sarah gave me the gold coins. I wouldn't have believed it had really happened if not for the letter written to me by Sarah, dated in the early 1900s, that I discovered when I returned."

Glaring at Josh, she emphasized, "But it did happen, and I have the proof."

"Are you saying that God sent you back in time?" Josh's voice rose, incredulous. "Really…to save someone who had been dead for almost a hundred and fifty years!" A twig snapped beneath his foot.

The sound brought his attention back to their surroundings. He came to an abrupt stop in the shadows beneath the canopy of newly budding leaves. "Em, this is ridiculous. We have to turn back now."

Ezra had not noticed that they had stopped and continued through the trees a few yards ahead.

"Excuse me, sir!" Em shouted. "Please, wait a moment."

Ezra turned to her with a look of disbelief at the word "sir."

Catching up to him, she lightly grabbed his arm. "Ezra, I'm sorry you got caught up in our troubles. Please, go back and pretend you don't know anything."

Ezra sighed as he removed his straw hat and wiped his shirt-clad arm across his brown forehead. He bowed his head slightly and spoke toward his feet. "I cannot, Miss Emily. Master Banister will have noticed that I have gone missing. If I am accused by Master Blackburn, I will hang."

"But what if he's dead?"

"I did not hit him hard enough to bring on death. Please, young master and miss, we have much ground to cover."

"Oh, no." Em closed her eyes and swayed on her feet. Both young men looked at Em with alarm.

Josh gently grabbed Em's shoulders. "Em, he doesn't know what he's saying. They don't hang people anymore. Besides he saved our lives. He's a hero."

"Ezra could die because of me."

Ezra flicked a glance at Em before focusing his eyes on the ground. "Now, Miss Emily, do not be anxious. I have a brother who was freed and lives in Boston. He can conceal me for a time."

Em's eyes, full of sorrow, looked at Ezra. "Are you sure?"

"Yea, Miss Emily. Now we must hasten to the river sloops in Petersburg before Blackburn awakens."

Josh opened his mouth, intent on stopping all this nonsense, but clamped it shut at the stricken look on her face.

"Please, no more stopping or questions until we get to Petersburg."

Under his breath, Josh mumbled. "But we are in Petersburg."

The three exhausted teenagers emerged from the woods on the outskirts of Petersburg. Josh and Em stared in shock. This was not the Petersburg they had driven through a few hours before. What they were staring at was a frontier town from some old-time movie, just a couple of narrow dusty streets parallel to the Appomattox River. The main road by the river was packed dirt. Visible on the right side of the river road were small wooden houses, a stable, a butcher shop with hanging carcasses, hog pens, and a two-story building with a sign out front that read "The Golden Ball Tavern." On the left were long warehouses with wooden docks that led down to barges swaying slightly in the river's current. Em wrinkled her nose as unpleasant odors drifted toward them.

"Young Master Joshua, do you perhaps have coin with you?" Ezra asked.

For the sake of his sanity, Josh refused to believe this was Petersburg. "If this is a joke, it has gone on too long." He turned to Ezra. "Are we on the set of a new movie being filmed on the Revolutionary War? Like *The Patriot*?"

Ezra said, "Master, I do not take your meaning. What is movie?"

Josh smiled and wagged his finger at Ezra. "Oh, you are good, my man. You both set me up good. What did you hit Blackburn with, a rubber axe head?"

Em groaned. "Ezra, I need a moment with Joshua."

Ezra stepped a few feet closer to the woods.

Turning to Josh, Em hissed, "We don't have time for you to bury your head in the sand and pretend this isn't happening. Men on horseback could show up at any time and arrest us for attempted murder, and then they will hang us. This is legit!"

Staring hard into Em's eyes, he could tell she was dead serious. She wasn't joking with him, and as much as he wanted to believe otherwise, she wasn't hallucinating.

Josh shook his head. "How am I supposed to believe the impossible?"

"Do you believe God can do anything?"

Josh did not hesitate. "Yes."

Em put her hands gently on Josh's cheeks and implored him to believe with her eyes. "I believe God sent me back in time to save Martha, and when you grabbed me, you came too."

Josh placed his hands atop Em's. After a moment he called to Ezra. "What year is it?"

Ezra strode back to them. Although puzzled by the question, he replied, "'Tis the year 1770."

Josh pulled Em's hands off his face, gripping them tightly as his own shook. He took a deep breath and squared his muscular shoulders. With a smile that trembled slightly on his handsome face, he whispered, "Okay."

Ezra's eyes widened at the unseemly display of affection between the miss and master but then were quickly cast downward as he addressed Em, "Do either of you perchance have coin?"

Em shook her head ruefully. "I'm afraid not."

"Without coin we will have to steal onto one of the sloops and conceal ourselves under the canvas."

Em's puzzled gaze followed Ezra's pointing finger where slaves loaded bundles of goods onto barges meant for trading to another colony. Not barges, sloops. The sun was shining bright overhead, and many of their dark-brown faces shone with sweat.

Em frowned. There was something significant about this year. And then it hit her, this was not America. All the colonies were still under British rule. As scared as she was, Em could not help but feel awed to be on the brink of America's independence.

Ezra was talking. "… need the cover of darkness to steal onto a sloop. We need somewhere to conceal ourselves until then. Isaac, at the stables, might be of assistance with our plight."

It occurred to Josh as he followed Ezra that he really was a slave and one that had run away. Remembering his history classes he knew that was not good, not good at all. Traversing beside Em down the narrow dirt and grass alleyway behind the plain wooden structure that housed the tavern, Josh joked, "We didn't plan well for this trip, honey. No change of clothes, no coin to stop in the local tavern and quench my thirst."

Keeping her voice low, Em said, "Hopefully, this will be a quick trip and we'll be back home tomorrow at the latest."

"How do you know?"

"I don't. I'm just going by what happened last time."

Josh reached down for a long grass blade poking through the dirt at his feet and stuck it between his lips. "And that was?"

"I helped to save Robert around three in the afternoon and came back to our time sometime that night while I was sleeping. When I woke up, I was blown away because although I had been gone for five days, I returned only thirty minutes after I had disappeared into the past. My mom had been searching the Petersburg house looking for me. She was really mad. She thought I was playing hide and seek."

"What day was that?"

"The day you surprised me at the old Petersburg house with ice cream."

Josh pulled the blade out of his mouth. "I remember that day. You went to that house with your mother to help her clean.

Megan and I felt bad that your whole Saturday was wasted cleaning, so we brought you the ice cream."

Ruefully, Em shook her head. "Trust me, the day was not wasted."

"Why didn't you trust me enough to tell me?" Josh said in a hurt tone.

Without saying a word, Em's glare said it all.

Josh gave Em a sheepish look. "If I couldn't believe you with the evidence staring me in the face, how would I believe you without it?"

Em took a deep breath and said, "Honestly, I didn't want to take the risk of you thinking I was crazy. We had only known each other for a few days."

Em smiled fondly in remembrance. "That was also the first time we held hands."

Josh entwined the fingers of his left hand with the fingers of Em's right hand. Two minutes later, Ezra paused at the large back doors of a stable. Indicating for them to stay outside, he cracked one door and slipped inside.

Josh dropped the blade of grass. "So let me see if I have this straight. You saved Martha, so..."

"We saved Martha."

"Okay, we saved Martha. So God should send us back tonight."

Em worried her bottom lip. "Yeah, but last time, I went and came back in the same house."

"No problem. We can ask Ezra to take us back tonight."

Em shook her head. "I can't ask him. If they catch him, he'll hang."

"Em, we don't know how to get back to Battersea. But I don't think it matters. If God did this, he can send us back from anywhere."

Before she could respond, Ezra stuck his head out the crack of the door. "You may enter, Miss Emily and Young Master Joshua."

Josh and Em entered the dim interior of the stable. The dirt floor was so dark it was almost black. High above their heads were large beams supporting an angled roof. A hayloft jutted out halfway between the ceiling and floor. Dust motes danced in the pale light that shone through the cracks in the wooden boards of the walls. The inside smelled not unpleasantly of hay and horse manure. There were four stalls on each side of the enclosure. Two were occupied by a bay and pinto. A stooped black man, with white wiry hair, stood next to Ezra holding a pitchfork in both hands. His leathery, wrinkled face was completely impassive. Having spent five days in 1865 with two freed Negros, Em understood that look. *Never let the white folks know what you're thinking.*

"This is Isaac. He cares for the stable. He said we can hide in the hayloft until night falls. His master has gone to Williamsburg for the week."

Em bobbed her head. "Thank you, Isaac, we are most grateful."

Josh took his cue from Em and bobbed his head also. "Isaac, would you have something to drink? Water?"

Wordlessly, Isaac pointed to a wooden bucket in the corner of the stable with a ladle above it, hanging on a nail. Josh and Em walked over to the bucket, and Josh lifted the ladle off the nail. Dipping a scoopful, he brought it to his nose and sniffed, before taking a cautious sip. His eyes widened in surprise.

"This is wonderful." He drank the whole scoop in one gulp and handed the ladle to Em.

Em drank, and a grin creased her lips. "Spring water."

Josh looked in the bucket. "Yeah, I bet it took at least two plastic jugs to fill that up."

"Josh! Remember where we are," Em whispered through her giggles. They each had three more scoops before their thirst was quenched.

Ezra pointed to the ladder attached to the hayloft. "Conceal yourselves in the hayloft. Isaac is going to find us some fare, and I will bring it up to you."

"Fare?" Josh asked as he climbed after Em.

CHAPTER 4

John Banister watched as Blackburn's eyes fluttered and then slowly opened. Although the room was dim with only the glow of the candelabra, his eyes still squinted as if the light was bright. Banister saw recognition in his eyes as he croaked out a question.

"Where...?"

"You are in my home at Hatcher's Run."

Blackburn tried to sit up and then grimaced in pain.

"Be easy, sir. You have quite a large knot on the top of your head. My dear wife, Elizabeth, has covered it with a poultice to help your pain."

Blackburn felt the rag-wrapped lump with his fingers.

"Do you perchance know the circumstance of your injury?"

Blackburn frowned in concentration. "I do not, sir."

"After my discourse with Mister Fletcher, I searched for you in the east wing. I found both you and Martha collapsed upon the floor of the last room. I hailed Mister Fletcher to see to Martha and had two of the day laborers carry your inert form to a wagon for transport to my home. It looked to me as if you had been accosted."

"How long was I insensible?"

"Since midday and it is nigh on evening."

Blackburn frowned in concentration. The last thing he remembered was talking to Banister about his villa. Sweat pooped out on his forehead as his head began to throb with pain.

"Relax, sir, no need to force a recollection," Banister said with concern. "I will have my wife bring you her homemade grog." He turned and departed the room.

Five minutes later, Mistress Banister bustled into the room with a pewter mug of beer, foam dripping down the sides. Setting the mug on the nightstand, she helped to raise Blackburn to a sitting position. With a kind smile she pressed the mug into his hands and left the room. As Blackburn sipped the heady brew, he relaxed against the pillows propped behind him and closed his eyes.

Blackburn's body gave an involuntary jerk, and his eyes popped open. With sudden clarity, the events of the day were revealed to him. *Why did Banister not know about the teens? The girl had been ready to run to him with her tale. They must have fled.* Blackburn frowned. *Neither had accosted him. Who would have dared such an act that assured the person a hanging?* Blackburn shook his head, which brought on more pain. His breathing quickened as his anger seethed. The mug he gripped trembled, and liquid sloshed over the sides and onto the coverlet of the bed. Blackburn barely registered a pounding at a door somewhere in the house as he took another large swig from the mug, foam covering his upper lip. Footfalls sounded and Banister entered the room with Mister Fletcher.

"Blackburn, Mister Fletcher has come from Petersburg, where I sent him to inquire of unfamiliar persons in the town. All of my Negros and laborers were accounted for. They were either chopping down trees or working in the west wing."

Mister Fletcher bowed. "Sir, the only strangers in town were noticed by Negros loading a sloop. A young lad and lassie accompanied by your Negro, Ezra. As they could not be the culprits, I did not inquire further."

Blackburn's eyes narrowed, but he kept silent.

Banister inquired, "They observed Ezra?"

A dark red mist covered Blackburn's thoughts. *The slave that had accompanied them from Williamsburg! If he was with the lad and lassie, he surely was the one to hit him on the head. No doubt an imprudent act of chivalry for the girl.*

"I would look to your Negro, Ezra, as the one who attacked me," Blackburn said definitely.

Twin looks of disbelief appeared on the faces of Banister and Fletcher.

"Sir, Ezra is my most valued slave. I know him well. He would not commit such a heinous act against your person."

Blackburn replied, "He is a runaway."

"He is not, sir. He is in Petersburg for a purpose that I shall be made aware of when he returns."

Anger turned into incredulity. "You allow your slave to leave your property without permission."

Affronted, Banister stated. "Whatever my dealings with my Negro, it is not your concern, sir."

Blackburn suddenly realized he could not afford to insult Banister. His face took on a mask of contrition. "I meant no offense. May I question him when he returns?"

"You may, sir."

Lifting the mug to his lips, Blackburn casually asked, "Have you word on the young servant girl?"

"Martha? She is in the care of Mistress Fletcher and has yet to speak."

Blackburn toasted his host with satisfaction. "To your good health, sir. I am in your debt."

Banister reached into the pocket of his waistcoat and pulled out an ornate knife. "I discovered this lying beside you in the room. Is it your blade? Did you perhaps use it to defend yourself?"

Blackburn feigned uncertainty. "It does look similar to the one I carry concealed in my boot. But I still have no memory of the incidence."

Banister laid the knife on the wooden nightstand. "I shall leave it here, and we will speak on the morrow after you have had a good night's slumber. Do you require anything before my wife and I retire for the evening?"

"I do not, sir." With a slight bow, Banister and Fletcher removed themselves from the room.

Blackburn took another swallow of his beer and belched. He paused in the act of setting the mug on the nightstand as the corner of his mouth quirked up in a smile. This misfortune could work to his advantage. Instead of using the ruse of interest in the home Banister was building, he could use the justification of talking to the laborers about his assailant to cover his search along the bluffs for the ledge. He needed to locate his father's hidden cache within the next few days. His creditors had become like hounds snapping at his heels, insisting on the payment of his gambling debts. His eyes narrowed to slits as he recalled Banister's defense of his slave Ezra. That Negro would pay with his life for assaulting him. He was satisfied that the teens would be too terrified to return to Banister's villa. He had put the fear of God in them. But Ezra's loyalty might cause him to return rather than run. He knew I did not witness my assailant. And when he did return... Blackburn slammed his empty mug down hard enough to rock the nightstand.

Blowing out the candle, he silently cursed himself for becoming distracted by the comeliness of the servant girl. But his thoughts did not linger on the girl. She would not utter a word against someone of his station. He had to find that ledge and the hidden opening in the cliff.

⸺≡◈≡⸺

As Blackburn schemed, Josh and Em devoured the meal provided by Isaac. They had not eaten since breakfast and were starving. The tin plates each held some type of sausage peppered with spices and cornbread. No utensils were provided, so Em ate with her fingers. She picked up the last bite of her sausage and savored the unique flavor. Em then plucked up the cornbread, taking a huge bite. It was moist and sweet and melted in her mouth. As she chewed, Em noticed that Josh had finished and was looking for something to wipe his greasy fingers on. Em reached into her pocket and pulled out the hankie with her blood on it and handed it to Josh.

"Kind of gross, but it's all we have."

Josh shrugged. "My mom has a saying, beggars can't be choosers. I guess that's us."

Josh handed the hankie back so Em could wipe her hands. Just as she finished, the upper portion of Ezra's body popped over the lip of the hayloft. He extended his right arm over and handed Josh the two tin cups he held.

"My apologies, 'tis water, Isaac has no cider or beer. If you have finished your supper, I will return the plates to Isaac."

"Please tell him how grateful we are for the food," Em said. "After you return the plates, could you come back up here so Josh and I could talk with you?"

"Yea, Miss Emily."

As he disappeared back down the ladder, Josh handed a cup to Em with a question in his eyes.

"We need to get directions back to Battersea. There has to be some kind of road so we don't have to go through the woods again."

Josh drank his water in two gulps and set the cup down beside him. "Even if there is, we'll never find it. Think about it. It's not like it would be an early version of Washington Street and lead straight there."

Em downed her water and let out a loud involuntary belch.

Josh grinned and raised his right hand. "That's a high fiver, Watkins."

Em smacked her right palm to Josh's with gusto. It made her think of the first time she had invited Josh over to dinner at her house. He had been stunned when her brother burped loudly on purpose and both Em's dad and Em said "All right" and high-fived him. Em's mom was trying to look disapproving but wasn't succeeding. It was obvious that no one high-fived burps during meals at Josh's house. But it took him no time at all to jump in, high-fiving Em when she was the next to burp. Her family was probably not the norm with this tradition, but it brought humor and closeness, even with her mother, who lectured about manners with a twinkle in her eye.

Bringing her thoughts back to what Josh had said, Em had to agree. The roads that existed in 1865, on her last trip through time, were nothing but wide dirt paths, except for the river rocks on Old Street. There had to be fewer roads now.

"Em, we won't make it back without Ezra. I think we should tell him why we're here."

As Em started to protest, Josh held up his hand. "Look, he thinks he's helping us by getting as far away from Battersea as he can. Nothing will get him to change his mind but the truth."

"Or," Em said, cynically, "he will believe we're nuts and take off. The slaves of this time period are very superstitious. Most of them continue to practice the religions of their home countries. You tell him and he is going to think we are witches. Well, that I'm a witch. You would probably be a warlock. Never mind. And if he has been converted to Christianity, he'll think we're demons."

"Okay then, why don't we go and find Colonel John Banister? Once we explain the circumstances, he should be delighted to let us stay at Battersea until God sends us back."

Em set her empty cup down and decided to ignore the sarcasm. "He's not a colonel, yet. The Revolutionary War hasn't started. Besides I've decided you're right and God will send us back from here tonight while we're asleep, okay?"

Ready with another witty comeback, Josh could only utter a perplexed "What?"

Ezra suddenly appeared, climbing over the last rung and standing deferentially in front of Em and Josh.

Em sighed. "Ezra, please sit down."

"Nay, miss, that would not be proper."

"Please, Ezra, it will hurt my neck, to look up at you."

Reluctantly, Ezra dropped onto the straw strewn across the wooden floor and stared at a spot between his shoes.

Before Josh could say anything, Em said, "Ezra, I know it is not considered proper to look directly at our faces when we talk to you, but you have our permission." Josh looked at Em quizzically, but said nothing. "We can't go with you tonight. Joshua and I must return to Battersea in the morning." Josh quirked an eyebrow, but Em rushed on. "There is a good reason, but we can't tell you right now. I'm sorry."

Shock filled Ezra's face as he raised it to Em's. *Why would they wish to return?* Ezra fought to get his emotions under control. It was not right for him to question a white girl. In a calm voice, he said, "Do not go back, Miss Emily."

Ezra had to make the young master and miss see the dire mistake of revisiting Master Banister's property. "Miss, it would be most unwise to return. You will be seen. Isaac informed me that Master Fletcher was in town inquiring about unfamiliar persons."

Em shook her head. "You should run, but Josh and I can't."

The decision to go or stay grappled like two wrestlers in Ezra's mind.

Seeing the indecision in his eyes, Josh said, "Ezra, I think we're all tired and scared, and maybe we should sleep for a few hours. Wake us up before dawn and maybe Em will have changed her mind."

Ezra descended the ladder to sleep in one of the stalls.

As soon as he was gone, Em hit Josh on the arm. "Why did you say that?"

"Because, hopefully, we'll be back in our own time when Ezra wakes up and he can conceal himself in one of the barges."

"Sloop."

Josh shoved his hands in the pockets of his breeches in exasperation. "Em, could you stop correcting everything I say?" Josh said.

"I'm sorry. I don't...don't know...why..." Tears were threatening.

Josh put his arms around her. "Shush, it's okay. Correct me anytime you want."

"I'm having a hard time dealing with what happened with Martha," she mumbled into Josh's neck.

"I know. Come help me gather this loose straw so we have something to sleep on."

Snuggled within Josh's arms, Em watched as the sun set and the sky turned into a beautiful canvas of pinks, yellows, and oranges through the large opening in the wall of the loft. Josh lightly kissed the top of Em's head and closed his eyes. Josh's breathing deepened as his body slipped into an exhausted slumber. Closing her eyes, Em prayed, *Lord, I don't want to seem ungrateful for the opportunity you have given me to save Martha, but could you please send Josh and me back to our own time. And please, Lord, protect Ezra so he does not hang. Amen.* Feeling calmer after her prayer, Em felt the day's tension leaving her body, and she slept. Neither she nor Josh stirred when the winds picked up and the rain pounded the roof of the stables.

It was still dark outside of the stables when Ezra gently shook Josh awake. Disorientated, Josh pushed at the weight against his chest. Em mumbled something in her sleep. At the sound of her voice, yesterday's events crowded his memory, and he stopped pushing.

"It is time we took our leave, young Master Joshua," Ezra said. Josh shook Em.

"Mom, it's still dark." Em waved her left hand in a shooing gesture.

Josh bent down close to Em's ear. "Em, we're still here, in the past."

Em sat up abruptly, rubbing sleep out of her eyes. She stretched her stiff legs. Her hair lay in tangles around her face. Em reached her fingers around to the back of her head and came away with a couple of bobby pins. Her bun had come completely undone, her auburn hair falling in tangled waves to her shoulders. She used the bobby pins to attach the mobcap more securely. As her eyes adjusted to the dark, she glimpsed Ezra throwing a leg over the lip of the hayloft and starting to descend the ladder. Josh helped her to her feet and held her hands as she lowered her right foot to the top rung. He followed after a few seconds. When they reached the bottom, Ezra led them through the darkness to the water bucket where each took a fortifying drink. Suddenly, Em had to empty her bladder in the worse way.

"Ezra, is there a privy nearby?"

"Privy, miss?

Great, it isn't called a privy in this century. "Ah, the place to relieve myself?"

"I am sorry, Miss Emily, I do not take your meaning?"

"Piss," Josh added helpfully.

The puzzlement on Ezra's face cleared. "Yes, miss, I will show you the way to the necessary house."

Em glanced sideways at Josh at they followed Ezra. "Piss?"

Josh shrugged his shoulders and grinned.

As they stepped through the stable door, a gentle rain dampened their hair.

"Great, it's raining," Josh stated, as he stepped in a small puddle.

"Isaac has head coverings I can borrow," Ezra stated.

The cloud cover obliterated the moon and stars so that Em couldn't see the hand she used to grip Josh's sleeve. Ezra led the way with Josh and Em right on his heels. When they reached the privy, Em entered first. Ezra and Josh huddled beneath a maple two feet away. Nature's call answered, all three stood under the maple for a moment and contemplated the weather.

"God is smiling on us with this blessed rain."

Josh was baffled. "Dude, it's like fifty degrees out and we're going to get soaking wet."

"Yea, but no one will be at their labors today on Master Banister's property."

Em shook her head. "Ezra, you can't take us back."

"In good conscience, I cannot let you travel there alone." Ezra's voice was firm.

"If you would revisit the stables, I will return momentarily with head coverings."

Ten minutes later, Ezra returned with two straw hats, similar to the one he wore. Draped over his arm was a homespun cloak for Em.

"Isaac's woman says you must wear this, Miss Emily, to keep the chill of the morning at bay on your journey."

Tears formed in Em's eyes. "Thank her for me, Ezra." Accepting the cloak, she continued, "Thank you for all your help. If you could just point us in the right direction, we'll start walking at dawn."

"I must accompany you to Master Banister's villa. Blackburn will tell Master Banister a falsehood to see that you hang. I am not a coward to conceal myself in hiding while you both perish."

"But you said that you would hang if accused. Josh and I can't let that happen, either."

"Stalemate," Josh piped in cheerfully.

Em glared at him, then turned back to their sacrificing savior. "Ezra…"

"Nay, miss, my mind cannot be altered."

The stubborn set to Ezra's mouth said it all. Em removed the bobby pins and the mobcap and shoved them in her pocket. Hastily she donned the cloak and settled the straw hat on her head.

"Lead on, my man," Josh stated as he clapped the straw hat down on his head, "I have your back."

The three teens stepped through the stable doorway and followed the alleyway back toward the woods. Deciding that Ezra needed to know everything, minus the trip through time, Em described what had happened after Ezra, Banister, and Blackburn had arrived at Battersea.

"Martha but fainted! 'Tis wonderful news. I feared that Martha had resisted Master Blackburn's advances and he had lost his senses and strangled her."

Em's vision from the day before filled her mind, and she shivered.

"There was talk among us slaves while the masters attended their meeting in Williamsburg. Master Blackburn's slave, Homer, said his master was the devil incarnate, bringing unsuspecting young misses to his home and taking their virtue right under his mama's nose. Mistress Blackburn had been bedridden since her husband passed away three years ago. When she heard women weeping, she would inquire about it to her son, but he told convincing lies about injuries to the house slaves. Mistress Blackburn knew nothing about her son's immoral games. But Homer said his mama had plenty of strength to scold him good about his gambling debts. Right before she died, two months ago, Homer could hear her hollering through three rooms that Master Blackburn would be the ruin of them."

Em was speechless with shock. Josh said in a deathly calm voice, "If he comes within ten yards of me and I can catch him, I'm going to beat the snot out of him."

"Snot?" Ezra said in bewilderment.

Shaking his head, Josh changed the subject. "Do you have a last name, Ezra?"

"Slaves have no surname."

"You and Blackburn both use Scottish terms. Are there a lot of sots, sorry, I mean Scots in Petersburg?"

With a quirky smile, Ezra said, "Both, Young Master Joshua."

Josh laughed. "All right, my man, high five."

Josh lifted his hand for a smack and saw the confusion on Ezra's face.

"Like this." Josh lifted Ezra's arm until their hands met. He gave it a light smack. "It's like a sign of approval."

Ezra shook his head ruefully. "Sometimes your phrases befuddle me."

"Right back at you. What does *befuddle* mean?"

"Confused." Ezra stopped at the end of the alley.

"And could you drop the master, it's kind of embarrassing."

"He can't, Josh. If he's caught only using your first name, he could be beaten severely," Em said, as the rain gently pelted her straw hat and cape-clad shoulders.

"Right, I keep forgetting where I am."

"We shall return through the woods. The thoroughfare would be too perilous."

Em glanced sideways at Ezra, "You speak very well, Ezra. Isn't that unusual for a slave?"

"My first mistress taught my brother and me to read, write and speak our words clearly. That is the reason Master Banister purchased me."

Ezra looked carefully around him before darting across the road and into the woods, Josh and Em at his heels. Once concealed within the security of the woods, Ezra stopped to listen. The only sound was the water dripping off the leaves above them. The branches of leaves were not thick yet, but still protected them from the majority of the rain. There was just enough light to see Ezra raise his finger to his lips in the centuries-old gesture of silence and then motion them forward on their trek back to Battersea.

Em's shoes squished as she walked. Muddy water had splashed inside them as she dashed across the road. Following in Josh's footsteps, she realized this was the first chance she had to really think about their situation since the horse's hooves had opened a hole in the floor. *Why didn't God send them back last night? Was she right and they had to be at Battersea to leave, or was there something else she and Josh were supposed to do first?*

Em's chest heaved with resentment. She hadn't asked to be a hero, and she didn't want to be one. *But,* a small voice in her head reminded her, *Martha would grow to adulthood because of her and Josh. Well,* she argued with herself, *that was good, but what about the fact that she was wet, cold, and utterly miserable?* Shivering, she tried to wrap the cape more closely around her. It wouldn't be long before she developed blisters from her wet boots. Em kicked a stick out of her path and decided it was her mother's fault. If she hadn't insisted that she and Josh volunteer for Battersea Days, they wouldn't be in this situation. She'd be curled up under her comforter, cozy and warm. Her breathing quickened as her anger built. Two days ago, just two days ago, everything had been fine.

CHAPTER 5

APRIL 2009

Em's eyes squinted at her image in the mirror as she pulled her auburn hair back in a ponytail.

"Em, Caleb, breakfast. Hurry, I don't want you to be late for school," Em's mom yelled up the staircase.

Entering the kitchen, Em was briefly bathed in the early morning sunlight that poured through the big bay window. Her mother, Elisabeth, was busy flipping french toast in the skillet.

"Honey, grab four glasses and pour the juice. Your dad has the day off."

Opening the fridge, Em pulled out the gallon container of juice. "Oh, yeah? So you're both playing hooky today."

"We have to take care of some business we can't do on the weekends."

After pouring the juice, Em's dad, Daniel, and brother, Caleb, entered the kitchen. Daniel kissed Elisabeth and Em on the cheek before sitting at the table. Elisabeth carried a platter of french toast and bacon from the counter, setting it on the tabletop before pulling out her chair. Once seated, Daniel blessed the food, and they took turns forking the toast onto their plates along with the bacon.

"Em, I got a call from Becky at the Colonel John Banister Chapter of the DAR. You've met her once. She's one of the teachers at my school," Elizabeth said.

Em swallowed a piece of bacon. "I don't remember."

"She's the one with the two-year-old little girl you thought was so adorable."

"Oh, yeah. What's the organization she's with?"

"Daughters of the American Revolution. It's similar to our Benevolent Ladies Society. They represent the Revolutionary War era, and we represent the Civil War era," Elisabeth said as she poured syrup on the toast.

"Anyway, she and her husband were supposed to dress in colonial period costume and volunteer at Battersea Days tomorrow, but her husband was in a car wreck two days ago and is in the hospital. She has called every member of her chapter, but they either already have plans or have already signed up for two-hour shifts. She called me in desperation, but your father and I have to help your Aunt Katy with her leaky roof tomorrow. Could you and Caleb help out for just two hours in the morning?"

Em's fourteen-year-old brother paused in the act of spearing another piece of toast. "Sorry, Mom, I have a soccer game in the morning."

Elisabeth contemplated her butter knife as she turned it back and forth in her fingers. "How about Josh? Do you think he might help you?"

"I didn't say I would help. It sounds really boring," Em said in exasperation.

"It's a very worthy cause. The house at Battersea is very historic, and the Battersea Foundation is trying to raise funds for its renovation."

"Josh and I had plans to shoot some hoops with our friends in the morning."

"It's only for two hours. Please, honey, it would mean a lot to Becky."

"Mom, I really don't..."

"How about a bribe? You can drive my car to school next week."

Em chewed on her lip. "All week?"

"If Marsha doesn't mind bringing me home."

"Oh, all right." Em heaved a theatrical sigh.

Early Saturday morning, Em left her bedroom at the same time that Josh emerged from her brother's room. He was dressed in a homespun white shirt, charcoal gray linen breeches, a worn-looking light gray vest, white stockings, and black buckled shoes. She was dressed in a light gray muslin dress with a built-in petticoat, white stockings, and black half boots with a white kerchief around her neck. Her mom had helped put her hair up in a bun and secure a mobcap on her head.

Josh grinned. "You look kind of cute, but those boots don't look right with your costume."

"Yeah, I know, the shoes didn't fit. And the dress is a little short. I guess they don't make too many costumes to fit women that are five ten like me. I'm just glad I didn't have to wear all the petticoats and stays. This dress has only one petticoat, and it's sewn in like a lining. It even has pockets and a zipper"

"The three-cornered hat's too small. And what's up with this shirt?" Josh's fingers plucked at each side. "It's so long, I had to tuck it between my legs just to pull on the pants."

"Breeches."

"Whatever. And the socks go up over my knees and are held up with little belts," Josh said with irritation. "Your mom so owes us."

"Repeat after me, only two hours."

"Em, honey, you better get going so you won't be late," Elisabeth called from the bottom of the staircase.

Josh drove his father's car over a set of railroad tracks and up to the metal gate at the bottom of a slight incline. At the top of the incline was sat a large white stucco house in need of repairs. A slender man in khakis and a green polo shirt showed Josh where to park. After parking and crossing over a shallow ditch, Em and Josh strolled hand in hand through the gate and toward the imposing house just past the circular driveway. Small white canvas tents were scattered over the landscape to the left and right of the drive. On the right a Union Jack flag flapped in the breeze. The other encampment flew the first flag of the United States with thirteen stars and stripes. Reenactors, some dressed as redcoats and others as patriots, strolled among the tents. The women reenactors were seated on three-legged stools before camp fires cooking the morning porridge in iron pots. Children in costume were playing with odd-looking toys. A young boy, his long brown hair pulled back in a queue, raced beside a large hoop he guided with a stick. A chestnut horse and her costumed owner stood to the right of the large house, the horse pulling up blades of grass and chewing contentedly.

Josh and Em climbed the wooden steps of the porch and approached a woman with a clipboard clutched in her hand.

"Excuse me?" Em said.

The women peered over the top of her clipboard and smiled. "May I help you?"

"Yes, we're the volunteers for the Colonel John Banister Chapter, Daughters of the American Revolution. We're supposed to help with a display table."

The woman adjusted her glasses and looked back down at her clipboard. "Let me see." Looking back up at Em, she said, "The DAR is in the far room of the east wing. They're setting up your table now." Holding out her hand, she said, "I'm Ann Thomas."

Em shook Ann's hand. "I'm Em and this is Josh. It's nice to meet you."

Josh smiled as he shook her hand.

Ann pointed with her pen. "Through the front door and turn right. It's the second room."

"Thank you."

Em and Josh crossed the threshold and turned right. Their footfalls sounded hollow in the empty room they passed through. The next room was also empty except for a folding table and two folding chairs.

A woman dressed in a long skirt, blouse, and vest with a mobcap on her strawberry-blonde hair was setting a cardboard box on the table. She turned at the sound of footsteps.

Em said, "Hi, Josh and I are here to help you this morning."

The woman held out her hand. "Hi, I'm Sally. Thank you so much for filling in at the last minute. I have to help with the wreath-laying ceremony, otherwise I would sit with you at the display table."

After shaking hands, Sally removed some pamphlets and flyers from the small box along with some period toys for children and laid them on the table. She explained that the pamphlets provided information on their Daughters of the American Revolution chapter and the personal history of the namesake for their chapter, Colonel John Banister.

"If you could hand these out to anyone who is interested, I would appreciate it. The toys are reproductions for the children to play with."

"Not a problem," Josh said.

"Great. Help yourselves to the lemonade in the west wing," Sally said as she walked toward the front of the house.

Em gazed around the room. It was very large with a high ceiling. The brick was showing through the plaster in a few places along the walls. The wooden floor planks were much wider and darker compared to the ones laid in her house.

"I'm going to hook us up with some lemonade," Josh said.

Em looked out of the window beside her, glad that she and Josh would be home before the battle started. Walking back to the table, she sat in one of the metal folding chairs hoping the next two hours would fly by.

CHAPTER 6

APRIL 1770

E m was jarred back to her new reality when Josh stopped in front of her and she walked into his back.

"Josh, why…"

"Shush. Did you hear something behind us?"

Em turned, but could see nothing through the gentle swaying of the branches.

"I don't see anything."

"I thought I heard something," Josh said.

From a couple of yards ahead, Ezra lifted his eyebrows in a questioning gesture. Josh raised his hand and waved him forward. Josh grasped Em's arm to help quicken her pace and catch up to Ezra. She was relieved to see that the rain had stopped.

Crack.

Ezra, Josh, and Em froze. Ezra put a finger to his lips and picking up his pace moved through the woods as quietly as possible. Em's breathing quickened. Josh's hand felt like a vise on her elbow as they hurried after Ezra. Another twig snapped, and although Em could not hear footfalls, her instincts told her she was being followed. Her heartbeats pounded loudly in her ears. *Was it Blackburn?* On the heels of that thought, Em heard a grunt, and her fears doubled. She had heard that sound before at the zoo in Chesterfield. It was the sound of a bear. Em glanced over her shoulder. She could see it, just a few yards behind them! Em screamed, and Ezra and Josh turned.

"Young Master, quick, put Miss Emily up that tree."

With no conscious thought, Josh lifted Em onto the closest branch of a large pin oak then turned to look for a weapon. Lying on her belly across the limb, Em reached above her to the next branch and tried to push to her feet on the lower branch, but the hem of her cape was twisted beneath her boots. Desperate, she tried to kick the hem free and lost her footing. Her tight grip on the branch above saved her from falling. Her arms, muscled and toned from months of basketball practice, allowed Em to pull her body up until her knees rested on the lower branch. She slung one leg over the branch so she could straddle it. She glanced down at the tense scene below her.

Ezra held a large rock in his hand, and Josh held a broken tree limb. The black bear, not as large as Em's fear-glazed mind had made him out to be, shook his shaggy, wet coat and sniffed at the air only a few feet from Josh and Ezra. He was very thin, and it occurred to her that he must have recently left his den after a winter of hibernation. Ezra shouted, startling Em, and threw the rock. If he intended to hit the bear, he missed by a foot. The bear backed up, stopped, and his black nose sniffed at the air again.

Agonizing seconds passed as Ezra, Josh, and Em waited to see what the bear would do. Growling low in his throat, the bear pushed himself up, in one fluid motion, to a standing position. And that was when Josh did what Josh did best. He dropped the stick and tackled the bear. Josh had a good two inches on the bear and plenty of momentum. He slammed into him, chest to chest, and they both went down. Rolling to the right, Josh regained his feet. Em couldn't tell whether Josh or the bear was more shocked by Josh's insane maneuver. Em guessed that after three years on the football field, his brains must be a bit scrambled. The bear shook his head once, flipped to his paws, and took off in the opposite direction.

As Josh helped Em down from the tree, she noticed the look on Ezra's face. As if Josh didn't have enough fans at the high school football stadium to worship him, now he had one here too.

With Em's feet safely down on the forest floor, she yelled at Josh, "Have you totally lost your mind? That bear could have killed you!" She had started to shake from head to foot with relief and anger.

Adrenalin still coursed through Josh's body as he bowed and said, "You're welcome."

"Oh, you!" Too frustrated to come up with a quick comeback, Em gave in to her feelings and threw herself into Josh's arms. "Please don't do that again," she whispered.

Josh wrapped his arms around Em's shoulders and held her tight until the trembling stopped.

"I didn't mean to scare you. All of a sudden I was so mad, I didn't think, just reacted."

"Right, like when you tackled Blackburn."

"Young Master Joshua, I have never witnessed such an act of bravery before." Awe laced Ezra's words.

"I have, when you nailed Blackburn with that axe to save our necks."

Em said, "I'm beginning to think you two have more brawn than brains."

"Brawn? Nobody says brawn?"

"I do, young Master."

Josh clapped Ezra on his shoulder. "Right, my man, forgot which century I was in for a minute."

"Josh!" Em glared at her boyfriend.

A thundering started in the direction the bear had disappeared. "More bears?" Em clasped Josh's left arm closer to her waist. "I do not believe so, Miss Emily. It sounds more like rain."

Within a minute, the heavens opened up and the rain pounded through the tree canopy above their heads. Within seconds Em was soaked. Her cape and straw hat offered little protection from the deluge that engulfed them. Ezra turned and started a slow jog through the wet woods.

Ezra stopped only once to retrieve the stashed axe. From the woods at the edge of Banister's property, he cautiously peered out at the house in the clearing. Motioning with the hand that held the axe, he moved toward the back of the property. Em did not notice a soul as they climbed the back stairs and entered the house. Once inside, she recognized that they were in the salon. Water dripped all around her from her hat and the hem of her cape. She started to shiver from the wet and cold.

"Your lips are blue, Em." Josh reached under Em's chin and untied the ribbons of her cloak, letting it fall to the floor. He lifted the sopping straw hat from her head and dropped it to the floor alongside the one he had removed from his head.

"Miss Emily, I will locate dry branches to build a fire in the hearth." Ezra disappeared through the door they had just entered, leaving it open.

"Ok-k-kay, we-e-e ju-u-u...st hav-v-ve to stay-y-y here," Em stammered as her teeth clicked together rapidly.

Josh pulled Em close and wrapped his arms around her.

Em sighed. "Your body's warm. Just like a little space heater."

Fifteen minutes later, Ezra staggered back through the door, his arms full of large and small branches. Josh rushed to help him with his load. Together they laid the smaller pieces for kindling in the hearth.

"There were quite a few dry branches close upon the house," Ezra said as he reached for a round tin container on the mantel.

Removing the lid he extracted a piece of rock, a short metal file, and a piece of, what looked like, burnt cloth.

"What is that?" Josh asked.

"It's a tinderbox," Em answered. "I've seen them used at the Civil War reenactments I've attended."

Ezra glanced up. "Civil War, miss?"

Em cringed as she realized her slip.

Before she could come up with a cover, Josh jumped in. "A game we played as children."

"Ezra, Josh and I will be right back."

Em grabbed Josh's sleeve and led him to the room where the display table had been before they disappeared into the past.

"We have got to watch what we say," Em said.

"I didn't say anything wrong.'

"You asked about the tinderbox. Every three-year-old in this time period knows what a tinderbox is for."

"Oh," Josh said, chagrinned.

"It's not Ezra I'm worried about. We could slip with someone who could become suspicious."

"But we're back at the house where we disappeared, or appeared or ah…time travel is confusing. Anyway, we shouldn't have to worry about that. You said we'll return to our time now."

"I don't know anything for sure, just what happened last time. I need to get back to the fire, I'm freezing in these wet clothes."

Em and Josh returned to the salon and welcomed the warmth of the blaze Ezra had burning in the hearth. Em sat on the floor and removed her boots and stockings, setting them beside the fire to dry along with her cape and hat. Ezra and Josh followed suit. Josh sat down behind Em and wrapped his arms around her waist. Gazing into the fire, Em's eyes filled with tears. They leaked over the edge of her eyelids, down her cheeks, and eventually on to her lap. One errant tear landed atop Josh's hand. He leaned forward and looked at Em's face.

Concern laced Josh's words. "Why are you crying?"

Ezra, noticing the tears, slipped out of the salon to give them privacy.

"Did you ever watch the *Wizard of Oz?*"

"Yes, it was one of my favorite movies when I was a kid."

Em tilted her wet face to Josh. Her lip trembled as she whispered, "I just want to go home. Why is God not sending us home?"

Josh kissed Em lightly on the forehead and whispered back, "I don't know."

Em buried her head in Josh's shoulder. "This trip back in time is nothing like the last one. Sarah, Abby, Rachael, and Moses took care of me and came to love me, despite the fact I had lost my memory and was a stranger who just appeared out of nowhere."

"You lost your memory? You didn't tell me that part."

Em leaned back against Josh's chest and told the tale of her adventure through time the year before in June. Josh listened silently for the most part, only interrupting to understand a point here and there.

"So almost the entire time you were there you had no memory of who you were, much less where you were. And you weren't scared, just determined to get your memory back. And when you did, you remembered the diary and Robert's murder. And with the help of Sarah, Moses, and William saved his life."

Em sighed. "Yes."

"And this time you knew immediately you had gone back in time, which would terrify anyone, and within thirty minutes you almost see a child raped, a knife is held to your throat, and your boyfriend is almost killed. Then you flee for your life, get soaking wet, and encounter a bear." Josh paused for effect. "Yeah, it is totally lame for you to want to go home."

Em laughed. "Well, when you put it that way."

Josh smiled as he placed his lips on top of Em's head.

"And there is one more thing that happened I didn't tell you." Em told Josh about the vision.

Josh's arms tightened. "Em, I'm such an idiot. You must have been terrified, and there I was going on about some theater production."

Em decided to voice what she suspected. "I think there is something else God needs us to do. That's why we haven't gone back yet. And that's what's scaring me the most, the unknown. I knew about Robert and Martha, but now I'm completely in the dark. I know I need to trust God's decision to leave us here. He proved how much he loves me with the last trip back in time."

"Then that is what we'll do, trust God," Josh said softly.

———◦———

Blackburn awoke to the pounding of rain on the roof above his head. Disoriented, he looked around his unfamiliar surroundings. A pale light was trying to push its way through the slats in the shutters covering the window of the bedroom. A sudden throbbing of his head brought his fingers in contact with his rag-wrapped head. The memories of the day before rushed back. He needed to return to Banister's property as soon as possible. Mindful of his tender head, Blackburn pushed himself off the bed. He stood up, the hem of his blouse billowing around his thighs. He reached for his stockings and breeches atop the chair next to the bed. As he pushed his arms into his coat, there was a knock on the door.

"Mister Blackburn, it does me good to see you up and attired. You do look less peaked than yesterday," Mistress Banister said as she set a tray on the nightstand. "I have brought you a mug of cider and cornbread to break your fast."

"Thank you for your kindness."

"With your permission, I will tend to your injury." Elizabeth unwound the linen bandage and examined the lump.

"It has decreased in size and has clotted nicely. I will inform my husband that you will join him in the dining room after you have partaken of a bit of sustenance."

Rolling up the bit of linen, Elizabeth left the room.

Blackburn paused before entering the dining room.

"Ah, Blackburn, you look splendid. Join me. Do you care for a glass of beer?"

Blackburn accepted the invitation and sat in the wooden chair offered.

"No beer, thank you. I quite enjoyed the mug your wife brought." Blackburn paused for a moment. "I am rather anxious to speak to your slave Ezra about the events of yesterday."

Blackburn noticed frown lines forming around the edges of Banister's mouth.

"Ezra has yet to return. 'Tis unlike him, I must admit."

The ticking of the mantel clock made Blackburn aware of precious minutes passing. "Very well then, if you could direct me to your property, I shall question those attending to their labors."

"I'm afraid no one is about. It is raining quite hard, and they will not be at their labors."

Excellent, Blackburn thought, *no one to watch me search.*

"Then the main road, sir. With your permission I shall return on the morrow."

Galloping down the muddy drive from Banister's house, Blackburn felt the tension from the last few hours leave him. He would locate the jewels and be back at his plantation before nightfall.

━━━◍━━━

Her dress finally dry, Em reached out and felt her stockings. She sighed with relief. She could cover her cold feet. Em turned her back to the boys and pulled the stockings up her legs, tying the ribbons of the garter to hold them up. Because a small blister was forming on the top of her left foot and her shoes were still damp, she left them off. Turning around, she noticed Ezra and Josh buckling their garters into place over their stockings. When Ezra turned away to stoke the fire, Em took a quick look at Josh's watch, which was still ticking merrily along in the eighteenth century. Noon. *Oh, how much longer, Lord?*

After another fifteen minutes had passed, Em pushed to her feet. She couldn't sit on the hardwood floor any longer; her rear end was killing her. She started to pace nervously around the room.

She stopped suddenly and looked at Ezra. "Ezra, thank you for bringing us back, but you need to get back to Petersburg."

"I shall stay with you and young Master Joshua until I know you to be safe."

"No, Ezra, please, you must...darn it, I need to use the privy...sorry, necessary house again. Is there one here, Ezra?"

Ezra rose to his feet. "I will show you, Miss Emily."

"That's okay; just point it out to me." Em winced as she put on her boot.

Em threw the cloak over her head as she left the shelter of the villa. She dashed to the corner of the building and then sprinted to the wooden outhouse only a few yards away. Had Em glanced left as she cleared the corner of the house, she would have seen a horse and rider turning onto the property.

Blackburn turned onto the drive to Banister's property and cantered down the muddy rutted road. He slowed his mount to a trot when he noticed the smoke rising from one of the chimney's atop the roof. Cautious, he left the drive and entered a grove of trees. He dismounted and looped the reins of the bridle over the nearest branch. Blackburn crept around to the back of the house satisfied that the steady rain would cover any noises he made. He peered through a pane-less window. The room was empty, so he moved toward the next window. His riding boots squished in the mud as he started to lean toward the window. He jerked upright as something creaked behind him.

Em pulled the cape up over her head and exited the privy. After taking one step, she froze at the sight of Blackburn standing next to a window at the back of the house. Reacting from pure terror, she screamed. Dropping the cape, she ran for the door to the salon not realizing that Blackburn could easily cut her off. As Blackburn did exactly that, she reversed direction and ran for the grouping of trees at the back of the property.

Hearing Em scream, Josh and Ezra flew through the back door and witnessed Blackburn chasing Em. Both took off at a dead run. Blackburn reached Em first.

"Halt or I will shoot the lad," Blackburn said as he lifted the flap of his oilskin cloak and pulled a double-barrel pistol out of the oversized pocket of his frock and cocked the hammer, being careful to keep the gun close to his body and out of the rain. Em stopped in her tracks a few feet from the tree line hugging the bluffs above the Appomattox River and turned around.

Ezra and Josh also skidded to a stop at the sight of the pistol.

"Bloody hell!" Blackburn fumed as he pointed the pistol toward Em and then back to Josh. "I would have thought you halfway to the Carolinas by now." Indicating his weapon, Blackburn continued. "I hold in my hand a double-barrel gun. One shot for each of you foolhardy teens if you move one muscle."

Em was silently praying for Ezra and Josh not to die at the hands of this lunatic as her insides quivered and churned in fear. She could see no way out. Certainly there would be no Ezra to save them this time. *Why had he come back to look for them?* Em tried to ease out of Blackburn's line of sight.

"Stop moving, lass." Em froze.

Blackburn looked at Josh. "Why have you returned?"

Em spoke, "We told you we are looking..."

"Do not take me for a fool!" Anger laced every word. "You have not returned for positions. Banister is not here. No one is about. What do you seek!"

Blackburn's eyes widened, and for a brief second fear crossed his features. But then the fear was almost instantly replaced with a countenance so fierce that Em could literally feel her feet shaking in her boots.

"Whereas you have immediately returned to this property despite the risk of arrest and hanging, I must deduce that you have acquired knowledge of...what I seek. Have you located my cache?"

"Sir, I don't know what you're talking about," Josh said as calmly as he could.

"Honestly, we don't know what you mean," Em pleaded.

"I shall have the truth!"

The sound of the rapids rushing below the bluffs penetrated the wrath seething inside Blackburn's head.

He motioned with the flintlock. "Proceed to the cliff's edge. The threat of a fall to the rocks in the river should loosen your tongues."

The three teens walked through the sparse pines to the edge of the cliff. Em felt faint and a bit dizzy as she looked down at the angry water. *Yes!* she thought, *this is it. God is sending us back now.* But instead of the dizziness increasing and turning into the familiar vertigo, the feeling subsided. She turned and looked back at Blackburn.

"I demand to know how you gained knowledge of my family's secret legacy or the lass will be the first to jump." Blackburn turned his body slightly to the left, leveling his weapon directly at Em's chest. Em's breathing quickened, and the sound of her heartbeats pounded in her ears.

"We don't know what you are talking about!" Josh shouted as his fear for Em made him desperate. Blackburn was too far away to tackle without the gun going off first, but he had to get the pistol's aim away from Em. He knew from school that these early weapons were highly inaccurate, so the odds were in his favor. He decided he would go in low for Blackburn's legs, now, before Blackburn's wrath exploded and Em was shot. Bending over slightly and tensing his muscles, Josh pushed off his left foot in a sprint for Blackburn. But before he could take two steps, Blackburn pivoted the weapon in Josh's direction and fired.

CHAPTER 7

Em screamed as she watched the ball from the pistol knock Josh back to the edge of the cliff. His footing faltered as the dirt at the lip crumbled beneath his shoes. In desperation, he reached out for the branch of a pine to his left, but it was too thin, and he could not get a grip. Flailing his arms, he plunged off the bluff toward the roaring waters below.

Ezra's fists clenched in rage as he craned his neck to scan the area below for the young master.

Em knees started to buckle as the horror of Josh's fall sank into her brain.

"Blast!" Blackburn's hand holding the pistol shook a bit as the situation he thought under his control dissolved.

"Come to me, lassie, or yon slave will suffer the same fate as your sweetheart."

Em turned to see the pistol leveled at Ezra's head. Em started to sob uncontrollably as she did as instructed. No one noticed that the rain had stopped and the sun was peeping through the clouds.

Blackburn grabbed Em's arm and glared at Ezra. "I see the truth now. 'Tis you that discovered my cache, while at your chores on the property. You enlisted the help of these teens to filch it and conceal it at another site."

Instead of the cowed demeanor Blackburn expected, Ezra stared in defiance at him.

"Nay, I have not discovered your cache."

Blackburn was enraged. "You insolent Negro!" The hand that held the pistol adjusted the aim an inch. "I had hoped to have the pleasure of watching you hang."

A split second before Blackburn pulled the trigger on his flintlock, Ezra leaped over the edge of the bluff. The ball whistled harmlessly over his head as he disappeared below the bluff. The shock of Ezra's jump stopped Em's wracking sobs. Desperation and adrenaline melded together as Em wrenched her arm free of Blackburn's hold. Whirling in a half circle, she raced away from the river and toward the back of the house, ignoring Blackburn's shout to halt. She knew it would take too long for Blackburn to reload his flintlock and shoot her, so if she could run faster than he could to the road, maybe she could find help. God would not allow Josh to die. He wouldn't. Still she prayed fervently as she flew up the two steps, thankful that the hem of her dress was above her heels so she didn't have to pick up her skirts. She rushed through the back door, slamming it just as Blackburn reached the steps. She could hear him wrestling with the latch as she hurried through the salon to the front door.

The latch refused to budge in Em's desperate fingers. Taking a breath, she stopped jerking on the latch and it released. She rushed through, slamming the door behind her again. She ran swiftly down the steps and sprinted beside the muddy track, her boots squishing in the grass. She glanced quickly behind her, but Blackburn hadn't made it through the front door yet. She mentally thanked her basketball coach for all the wind sprints she made her do. Em reached the road and turned left.

Blackburn stared stupidly at his empty hand and then with grim determination sprinted after the meddlesome girl. He had almost apprehended her at the back porch, but she slammed the door in his face. It took precious seconds before the black latch gave way, and he rushed through to the front door, only to find it also latched. Furious, he slammed his hand down on the handle to release the catch. But when he pushed on the door, he discovered it to be stuck. He backed up and took a few quick steps before using his shoulder as a battering ram into the left panel on the door. The door flew open and crashed against the house. He could see the girl halfway to the road running almost at the speed of a young colt. He couldn't give chase on foot and hope to catch her. He dashed off for his horse hidden in the trees. Mounting in one smooth motion, he gave his stallion's withers a fierce kick, galloping toward the road.

Blackburn yanked on the reins as he reached the end of the drive. He glanced in both directions, but there was no sign of the girl. *What was he to do with her?* He had no doubt that he would apprehend her. *Should he murder her and dispose of her body in the woods?* But even as the thought crossed his mind he shook his head. He needed her alive. She would know the location of the gems, if they had been moved. He would take her back to his plantation and lock her in one of the rooms. Once he had secured the jewels, he would decide her fate. Jerking the reins to the left, he set his horse to a steady trot toward Petersburg, glancing in the woods to the left.

Josh's still body lay face up on a ledge halfway between the lip of the cliff and the river below. Ezra sat near Josh's head praying to the white folk's God. He had been told by his last mistress that their God was the God of slaves too, but he seemed so very far away. And why would he listen to the plight of a slave? Nevertheless, he prayed for the young master to awaken and not succumb to any injuries as the result of his fall.

Ezra's heart soared when he saw young Master Joshua's eyelids start to flutter in a rapid motion. He looked up toward heaven and whispered his gratitude.

Josh opened his eyes and tried to focus them. A hazy brown ball with eyes wavered in front of him. Each eyelid felt as if it had a weight attached to it as he tried to blink the object into focus. It was a face, actually two of the same face weaving in and out of focus, but he couldn't place it as one familiar to him. The lips were forming words, but he could not hear them over a loud roaring.

Josh tried to rise, and then groaned as pain split his head in two.

"Nay, young Master Joshua, do not move. You tumbled off the bluff."

Ezra leaned in close to hear over the roar of the water as Josh whispered through his stiff lips, "Where am I?"

"You are on a ledge that broke your plunge to the river." Ezra gave a sigh of relief. "It does me good to see you have awakened."

Josh closed his eyes again because of the pain in his head and tried to make sense of what the black man had said to him. *A ledge? Above a river? What river?* Minutes passed before Josh opened his eyes again to the two faces.

"Do I know you?"

"I am called Ezra." Although he had never dared do it before this moment, Ezra grasped Josh's hand in his and squeezed it in reassurance.

Josh closed his eyes again. More minutes passed as Ezra sat patiently beside Josh holding his hand. As the pain lessened in his head, a name seemed to whisper through his brain.

"Em." He did not realize he had said the name out loud until Ezra questioned him.

"Young Master?"

Josh's eyes flew open with panic. "Em, where's Em?"

Memories were rushing back through Josh's mind at a speed that caused his head to pound again. He remembered Blackburn and a gun trained on Em, but nothing else after that.

Regret laced Ezra's words as he shouted above the roar. "I know not, young Master Joshua. Master Blackburn tried to dispatch me with his pistol after you fell. I leaped off the cliff and grabbed yon sturdy sapling." Ezra indicated the pine tree growing out of the bluff a few feet above the ledge.

"I remember you now. You tried to help Em and me."

Josh's struggled to rise. "I have to find Em." A stabbing pain to the left side of his abdomen forced him to stop.

"Nay, young Master Joshua, do not try to rise."

"My side feels like I got hit by a sledgehammer." Josh twisted his head to look down at his side—two sides. The double vision was really annoying. He probably had a concussion. And it wouldn't be the first time. He could see a small round hole in his vest pocket.

"Master Blackburn shot you and you fell from the cliff. The ball hit a strange object in the pocket." Ezra picked up the item he had placed on the ledge beside him. "It stopped the ball from the pistol."

Josh gazed in amazement at a small flattened piece of gray metal embedded in his cell phone.

Despite his whole body aching, Josh laughed. "My mind is totally blown. I can't believe my cell phone saved my life. I don't even remember putting it in my vest pocket. I thought it was in my breeches pocket."

The grin disappeared as Josh's thoughts turned back to Em.

Josh's mouth trembled as he voiced his worse fear. "Do you think he shot Em?"

"Nay, he had but two shots in the pistol."

"But I remember, he had a knife." Josh tried to push up again, but his double vision started to go gray, and beads of sweat popped out on his forehead. He dropped his head back to the ledge.

Josh had never felt so helpless before. His fear for Em was tying his gut in knots. He looked up at Ezra in desperation.

"Please, Ezra, leave me here and search for Em."

"I did not want to depart until I was sure you would awaken. I feared that you would turn over and fall off the ledge."

"Please, Ezra, go," Josh begged.

Ezra jumped up and absently shoved the damaged cell phone into his breeches pocket as he grabbed the lowest branch of the sapling. Once he had a good grip, he pulled himself up until his chest rested on the branch. Ezra inched his chest farther over the branch until he had the leverage to flip around and straddle the limb facing the cliff. Reaching above him, he grabbed the next branch and rose to his feet. He tried to repeat his first maneuver, but the upper branch had too much give because he had grabbed it earlier to save his fall. He reached to his right and tried to get a grip on the bedrock, but it crumbled beneath his fingers. He glanced up, but the edge of the cliff was a good three feet above him. Carefully, he descended to the floor of the ledge.

"I shan't be able to ascend, so I must descend."

Josh looked below at the rocks and roaring water eight feet below. "No, that would be suicide."

Every fiber of his being fought the next words he uttered above the roar of the water below. "We'll have to wait until the construction crew returns tomorrow and yell for help."

Ezra shook his cropped head. "Nay, young Master Joshua, no one would hear our cries of distress over the bellow of the river."

Josh groaned in frustration. He looked up at Ezra. "Are you a Christian?"

Ezra replied, "I am a believer of the Good Book, baby Jesus, Mother Mary, and our Creator who watches over his children. My first mistress used the Bible to teach me to read."

"Please help me to pray for a miracle. We are going to need one."

Ezra bowed his head.

Josh closed his eyes and spoke loudly, "Please, God, we need another miracle. I know it was a miracle by your hand that stopped the bullet with my cell phone, and broke my fall to the river with this ledge. You are an awesome God, and I am filled with awe because of your love for me and Em. Please keep Em safe wherever she is right now and help Ezra and me to get off this ledge."

"Yea, Lord, amen," Ezra finished.

"Thank you, Ezra." Josh brought his wrist up close to his face. He sighed with relief. At least his watch hadn't broken in the fall. Four o'clock. When Em had looked at his watch right before she went to the outhouse, it had been noon. He frowned in concentration. He had been out for almost four hours. His stomach clenched again at his fear for Em. He had to get off this ledge.

CHAPTER 8

E m stepped away from the tree she had been hiding behind as she watched Blackburn trot down the road toward Petersburg. It looked like her ruse had worked. Counting on Blackburn witnessing her left turn at the road, she had immediately abandoned the road and concealed herself behind the trunk of a large tree. Em turned right heading in the opposite direction. She paused beside the dirt track to Battersea and gazed at the house. She set one booted foot on the rutted drive. No, she couldn't. When Blackburn didn't spot her on the road or in the woods beside it, he would immediately look for her back at Battersea figuring she would try to find Josh. She had to think positively. Ezra could have survived the jump and was helping Josh. Steeling herself from the doubts that tried to creep back into her thoughts, Em turned back to the dirt road and started running, trying to avoid the puddles. She was bound to find someone who could help her.

After a mile, her run had slowed to a walk, and thirty minutes later, Em was limping badly. She wanted to scream each time the top of her boot scraped the blister. There was no choice; she was going to have to go barefoot. Spying a large rock, Em sat down and removed both shoes and stockings. She shoved the stockings into the muddy boots and then shoved the boots into the large pockets of her dress. She bent down to examine the blister. The blister had popped, and the skin was rubbed raw.

"Good luck finding Neosporin and a Band-Aid in this century," she muttered.

Her head jerked upright at the sound of clip-clopping hooves. Moving quickly, she hid behind some trees. She peered through the branches as two large mules harnessed to a wagon came into view. A young woman and a boy of about twelve years sat slightly slumped on the wooden seat. Em tried to conceal her disappointment that it wasn't a man driving as she came out of hiding.

"Good day to you," Em said as she remembered the greeting that had floated through the door as she and Josh manned the display table.

"And to you, miss," the woman replied as she pulled on the reins.

"I am in desperate need of a man's help. Josh and Ezra have fallen from the cliffs behind a house that is being built down the road a bit." Em's words carried more than a hint of desperation.

"Is there no one on the property to assist you?" the woman replied.

"Nay, the rain kept all the laborers away." Em slipped easily into the nuances she had picked up from Ezra.

Em lifted her hands toward the woman. "Please, I am so afraid they could be badly hurt."

"Mama, I can help her search." The youngster turned to his mother with eagerness.

"And a fine help you will be, but we must get your papa's assistance also. Slide closer to me so the girl can climb aboard."

A footrest protruded from the side of the wagon, and Em place her bare foot on it as she grabbed the wooden bench seat and hauled herself into the wagon. The woman tilted her head a little as she realized that Em was extraordinarily tall for a woman. Embarrassed that she was staring in a rude manner, the woman cast her eyes toward the mules and yanked the reins hard to the right to turn them back in the direction they had come. The mules moved out at a fast gait, eager to return home. Em noticed that the woman wore the more common long skirt, blouse, and vest she had glimpsed the women wearing at Battersea Days. Instead of a mobcap, she wore a cap in the shape of a sunbonnet with the two ties dangling on either side of her neck. Wisps of mousy brown hair peeked out beside her ears. She looked to be close to forty, but Em had read about how harsh life was in this time period, so she could be much younger.

"My name is Emily," Em said.

"I am Mistress Adams, but you may call me Rebecca. This is my son, Daniel."

"I am very pleased to make your acquaintance." Em paused and then continued,

"Is your husband close by?"

Rebecca clucked to the mules. "He is at our farm a little farther up the road attending to our newly planted crops."

Em rubbed her hands together in her lap and tried not to break down in tears again.

"Where are your shoes?" Daniel was staring at her feet in dismay.

Em tried to curl her toes up under her dress. "They are in my pockets. I have a blister on top of my left foot."

"I will attend to it when we arrive home," Rebecca said in a businesslike manner.

Five minutes later, the mules turned down a rutted track, similar to the one at Battersea. But Rebecca's home was nothing like the colonel's. The structure was one story and constructed with logs. Similar to pictures she had seen in her history books. The one pane-less window had open shutters, and Em could see homemade muslin curtains fluttering. Rebecca brought the wagon to a stop, and Daniel brushed past Em as he hopped down.

"I'll go find Pa," he shouted as he raced around the dwelling.

Rebecca and Em exited the wagon. Rebecca looped the reins around a hitching post as the mules stomped and blew their displeasure at not being unhitched. Em followed her through the doorway of the house. Their home consisted of one large room and a loft. Rebecca disappeared through a large curtain hung on the right side just behind the ladder to the loft. Em let her eyes roam the room. There was a fireplace embedded in the wall opposite Em. Two rockers and a straight-back chair sat before it. A worktable occupied the space directly beneath the front window. A wooden table and two benches sat in the middle of the room on the left side of the room. A cabinet with tin plates, cups, and crude eating utensils sat against the rear wall. A spinning wheel sat beside the fireplace. She had seen one in a museum her family had toured the year before. She knew it was used to twist the flax fibers into thread to make the clothing of this century. At odd moments like this, it would hit her that she really was in another century. Her body started to shake with a delayed reaction from the trauma she had endured.

Rebecca emerged from the behind the curtain with a piece of cloth and a small tin container in her hand. Noticing the trembling of Em's body, Rebecca hurried to her side and grabbed one of Em's hands with her own.

"Please, Emily, do not distress yourself, my husband, Jonathan, will find your companions."

"I'm sorry, I feel a little faint." Em swayed as lightheadedness overcame her.

Rebecca let go of Em's hand and wrapped her arm around Em's shoulders as she supported her to the chair so she could sit down. She eased her down and dashed to the water bucket beside the worktable, dipping the linen cloth in the water. She set the small tin can down to wring out the cloth. She rushed back to Em and pressed the cloth to Em's pale forehead.

"Lean your head back, Emily."

Em did as she was told and waited for the tremors and lightheadedness to pass.

"I will attend to your foot."

Rebecca reentered the curtained alcove returning with another strip of cloth. She retrieved the tin can and kneeled beside Em's left foot. She removed the lid and with two of her fingers dipped a portion of the thick salve out and, brushing aside Em's dress, placed it on top of the blister. A minty scent reached Em's nose.

Em leaned forward. "What is that?"

Rebecca wrapped the linen strip around Em's foot. "It is a poultice of sorrel, rum, willow bark, and mint. It will help the wound heal quickly." Rebecca tied the ends of the strip together and rose from her knees.

Rebecca's mouth turned down in a concerned frown. "Your skirt is damp and muddy. Were you caught in the rain? Have you broken your fast?"

It was Em's turn to frown. *Broken my fast?* But then her forehead smoothed out as the meaning of the phrase came to her. It had been used by Sarah and Abby. "I haven't eaten anything since yesterday. And I was pretty much drenched."

"I will build up the fire so you may dry your skirts."

The dizziness and shaking had stopped, and her stomach rumbled at the thought of food. Her father said she could eat any boy under the table with her appetite.

Rebecca walked over to the fireplace. She added wood to the shimmering orange coals and coaxed the fire to a bright blaze under a cast-iron pot. She then left the house only to return a few minutes later with a large crock pitcher. Rebecca sat the pitcher on the dining table with a plate of cornbread then reached into the cabinet and removed eating implements. Crossing to the fire, she stirred what was in the pot. Em hoped whatever it was would be eatable. After a few minutes, Em heard a plop followed by another as Rebecca stirred. Satisfied, Rebecca swung the pot off the fire by the black hook it hung on. Rebecca motioned for Em to sit at the table. Fetching a wooden bowl off the table, Rebecca spooned a cream-colored mush into the bowl.

Em's face wore a smile. "Porridge."

Rebecca poured milk from the jug into a tin cup. Em took a cautious sip and grinned. "This is nice and cold."

"It does keep quite cold in the cellar," Rebecca said.

As Em began to eat, Rebecca asked how her companions had fallen from the bluff. Before Em could reply Daniel rushed through the door followed by a thin man with brown hair that waved to his shoulders. He clutched a straw hat in his large knuckled hands. Em started to rise.

"Nay, finish your meal, a few minutes more will make no difference to the fate of your companions."

The two males in the room didn't speak as she finished her meal and rose from the table. Glimpsing her bare feet, she reached into her pockets for her stockings and shoes. Her shoes were wet and the stockings damp. Rebecca reached over and felt both.

"Nay, Emily, you cannot wear these. You will acquire more blisters. I will place them before the fire.'

Em's stomach started to clench in fear. "But I must go and find Josh and Ezra."

"Jonathan and Daniel will go and search if you can instruct them as to the location of the accident."

Though frustrated, Em knew she was right. She could not afford more blisters. She quickly explained in detail where to find the boys. Jonathan gave a brief bow and exited the house with Daniel.

"Please, Emily, sit in the rocking chair where you will be more comfortable while you wait."

Rebecca's brown eyes were full of sympathy as Em settled in the rocker to wait. She gazed into the fire and prayed silently. *Please, Lord, let them find Josh and Ezra.*

———◦◉◦———

Blackburn's anger and frustration were growing. The girl was not on the road, and he had searched into the woods on both sides with no sight of her. Could she have somehow slipped past him as he searched one side of the thoroughfare? He had seen her turn left at the entrance to the road. The leather of his saddle creaked as his horse pranced in place with impatience. His scalp itched under his tricorn, and he wondered if the lice were back to plague him. Blackburn glanced down the path to Banister's new home. Could she somehow have tricked him and doubled back to the cliffs. As he pulled on the right rein, a wagon came into view, the mules pulling hard in the harness.

The wagon driver yelled "Whoa" and sawed the reins as the wagon drew even with Blackburn. "Good day to you, sir."

Blackburn responded, "And to you. What brings you to the property of Mister Banister?"

Jonathan had not expected to run into a gentleman and was a bit disconcerted. He pointed to the house under construction. "My wife encountered a young girl upon this road who is afeared for a companion and slave who have fallen from the bluffs behind this property. I have come to search for them."

Blackburn's body went rigid. "You say they fell from the cliffs?" He thought furiously as the man answered.

"How many years would this girl have?"

"A teen, maybe fifteen years."

Blackburn hid his excitement. "A comely lass, with reddish hair and quite tall?"

"Aye. Do you know her then?"

"I do indeed. She is my indentured servant and a runaway. Her companion and the slave are also my property." Blackburn did not have to fake his rage as he answered. "The lass, lad, and slave filched some coins and disappeared yesterday. Banister has given his leave to search his property. But I would see to the lass first. Where is she?"

Jonathan was a kindhearted man, and given the opportunity he would have helped Emily run from the likes of this gentleman. Masters could be quite cruel to their servants as he knew from firsthand experience. He had been indentured for four years and had run himself when the ship he had worked on docked in Charles Town harbor. Jonathan's fingers tightened on the reins. He had no choice; the angry gentlemen was waiting for him to disclose the whereabouts of his property. If he lied, he could end up at the gaol in Williamsburg.

Resigned, he answered the gentleman's question, "She is at my home. If you would follow me, I will take you to her and then return and help you find the boy and Negro."

Blackburn shook his head. "That will not be necessary. Once I have acquired the girl, Banister's servants will help me locate the other two."

CHAPTER 9

The searing fire had dried her stockings. Em rolled one down and inserted her foot for the second time that day. Her boots were propped up on an iron bar facing the flames. It was some sort of contraption made to help dry the leather inside her boots. Shoes must get wet a lot in this century, Em mused as she finished tying the ribbons on both stockings.

"Your ankle shoes are almost dry," Rebecca said after feeling inside one of Em's footwear.

Em's eyes moistened with tears. "I can't tell you how grateful I am for your family's help."

From her kneeling position, Rebecca reached up and took one of Em's hands. The braying of a mule caused both women to glance toward the door.

"But it can't be your husband. He hasn't had time to search," Em said.

Rebecca rose in one swift motion and reached above the fireplace mantel for the musket that hung on two pegs. Cautiously, she made her way to the window. Peering around the corner, she gave a sigh of relief and laid the musket on the worktable.

"'Tis my Jonathan and a strange gentleman."

Anxious as to why they had returned so soon, Em turned in the rocker toward the door. Jonathan held the door open and bowed for someone to enter. Blackburn's menacing presence filled the doorway. Em jumped up from the rocker, sending it rocking back and forth rapidly. She backed away in fear, coming too close to the glowing embers scattered in front of the dancing flames. The hem of her dress brushed against one of the embers and started to smolder. Rebecca noticed the smoke rising from the hem of Em's skirt. She grabbed a straw broom propped at the end of the mantel and frantically began to beat at the smoldering hem. Em stood stunned between the two dangers unable to move. Rebecca dropped the broom after extinguishing the threat and pulled Em away from the fire.

"My goodness, Emily, you're as white as my linens," Rebecca said.

"Is this your servant, sir?" Jonathan queried.

"'Tis indeed the lass I have sought," Blackburn replied grimly.

Em shook her head violently as she tried to speak past frozen lips. Rebecca glanced at her husband, but dared not voice the question that came to her mind.

Blackburn realized he now knew the meddlesome girl's name. "Come to me, Emily. You shall get the lash for running."

Em spoke through her shock, "No, no, he's lying. I'm not his servant." She looked to Rebecca in desperation. "He shot my boyfriend and he fell from the cliff, and then he tried to shoot Ezra, but he jumped. He..."

"Cease your deceitful prattle, lass. These good folk shall not be affected by it."

He took a step toward Em, who ran in her stocking feet to the ladder attached to the loft in a desperate bid to escape. She had only climbed two rungs when she felt a strong arm encircle her waist and lift her off the ladder. Em struggled as if her life depended on it.

"Stop fighting me or I will enlist the aid of this field planter and bind you to the back of my horse."

Bind? Em stopped trying to get away. If he tied her up, her chances to escape would diminish greatly. Breathing heavily, she jerked free of Blackburn's arm. He roughly clasped her right wrist and pulled her to the door of the cabin.

"A moment, sir," Rebecca called, "the girl's shoes."

Rebecca lifted the boots from the fire and placed them before Em. Em tried to get the right one on one handed, but couldn't. Blackburn released her wrist. Although dry she struggled with the left boot because her foot was still wrapped in the linen cloth. Blackburn grabbed her wrist again and dragged her to his horse.

"Mount," Blackburn ordered.

Frustration seethed through every pore as she put her foot in the stirrup. Blackburn grabbed her waist with both hands and practically threw her into the saddle. He was definitely stronger than he looked. In one fluid motion, he mounted behind her. Em had little more than a couple of seconds to express her gratitude toward the Adams family before Blackburn turned the horse's head toward the road.

"Thank you for your kindness. I'll never forget it."

Jonathan and Rebecca nodded their heads in acknowledgement, while Daniel stared at her in confusion. Blackburn wrapped an arm around Em's waist and kicked the horse sharply in the withers. Em grabbed the mane and held on for dear life as the horse galloped down the soggy lane. At the roadway, Blackburn yanked on the right rein, and the steed thundered down the muddy road in the direction of his plantation.

⸻

The sun had dipped way below the horizon and the sky had faded from orange to lavender when Josh finally felt strong enough to sit up. Ezra got an arm under Josh's shoulders and pushed him upright. Josh leaned over holding his head in an effort to stop the spinning. He glanced at Ezra just as his face solidified into one image.

He cleared his throat and said "Thank the Lord, the double vision's gone" in a voice loud enough for Ezra to hear him.

Ezra shouted back, "What is double vision, Master Joshua?"

"Well, my man, I was seeing two of everything for a while. I probably have a slight concussion, but nothing I haven't suffered before on the football field."

"And what is a football field?"

Josh hesitated before answering.

Ezra cast his eyes downward. "I apologize, Master. I am being disrespectful, asking too many questions."

It was something about Ezra's downcast eyes that caused something inside Josh to clench in sorrow. He was the same age as his best friend, Tim, who was also black. Ezra should be playing basketball or whatever teens did in this century. And the master thing had to go. There was only one master of this world past or present, and Josh wasn't him.

"Ezra, I need to tell you a story about Em and myself, but I have to ask a question. Do you believe the stories in the Bible about the creation and the miracles Jesus did?"

Ezra's eyes widened. "Yea, Master Joshua. 'Tis God that made the heavens and the earth."

"Good, I need you to listen carefully to a miracle that happened to Em and me yesterday."

The sky overhead darkened to violet and the moon and the stars appeared as Josh explained how he and Em had come to be at Battersea. Ezra listened intently, no emotion showing on his shadowed features as he leaned in to hear over the roaring waters. Josh finished his tale and waited on the verdict. Either Ezra would believe or he wouldn't. Ezra placed his hands on his thighs and stared up at the moon and stars. Slowly he pulled his eyes from the night sky and looked at Josh. "I believe you, Master Joshua. I have seen many a person who has lost their senses, and you are not one of them." Ezra pointed at the round hole in Josh's vest pocket. "Who but God veered the bullet from your heart to the strange object from your time?"

Josh struggled with an emotion in stark contrast to his tough athletic persona. He brushed at the wetness in his eyes with the sleeve of his blouse. "Thank you." Josh shifted his legs into a more comfortable position and spoke into the darkness, "Ezra, please don't call me master anymore, it makes me uncomfortable. In my time there are no slaves. All the white and black people are equals, and many have friends and family in common."

It was too dark to tell, but Josh got the sense that Ezra was in total shock.

"No slaves, mas…huh…Joshua…and Quakers in common?" Disbelief was clear in his voice.

"Quakers?" Josh's voice was puzzled.

"You said friends. Quakers address each other as friend."

"Oh. I don't mean Quakers. In my time a friend is someone you care for, like my best friend, Tim."

Ezra voice was full of awe. "'Tis hard to comprehend… Negros and white people are equal."

"The president of this country is half white and half black," Josh said.

"What country? And what is a president, Joshua?"

"Just call me Josh, like Em does. Okay, I know this a lot to take in at once, but a war is coming to these colonies in the next few years. The men and women of the colonies will fight the British soldiers for control of the colonies, and they will win, in the year 1781, I think. All of the colonies become states under one nation called the United States of America. The general who led the colonies' army will become the first president of the nation, George Washington."

Ezra shouted above the roar, "Master George Washington! I know of him. He talked with Master Banister a number of times when we trekked to Williamsburg on business. 'Tis so extraordinary! I have many questions."

"Looks like I have plenty of time to answer them, but could it wait until morning? I have a headache from shouting."

Yes, M...Joshua, ah, Josh."

"Great, dude. I'm going to lie back down and try to grab some shut-eye."

"I will watch over you, I am too excited to seek slumber."

Josh tried to adjust his sore body on the hard ledge as he stared up at the moon. *Hang in there, Em, wherever you are. I'll find you.*

———◦◦◦———

Blackburn paced the library of his home in Dinwiddie County. Pausing beside the fireplace mantel, he lifted the brandy snifter to his lips and downed its contents. The pounding was fraying the last of his nerves. The girl had been beating on the door off and on since the moment he had shoved her into his mother's room and turned the key in the lock. He needed to think. Slamming the glass on top of the mantel, Blackburn spun on his heel, left the library, crossed the short passage to his mother's bedroom door, and slammed his fist against it.

"Leave off the pounding or you shall have no supper!"

"You shot my boyfriend!" Em shouted.

"And I shall do the same to you if you do not leave off and let me think!"

The sound of weeping reached his ears, but the lass no longer beat upon the door. Blackburn returned to the library. Before he could shut the door, his Negro, Homer, appeared in the doorway.

"Pardn' me, Masta', but Hattie asks if supper be served now?"

His first reaction was to summarily dismiss the slave, but then he reconsidered. He had not eaten since breaking his fast that morn at Banister's home, and he was hungry.

"Yea, and bring a plate to the lass in your late mistress's bedroom, but mark my words, if she escapes, the lash will caress your back too numerous times to count."

Homer swallowed hard before replying, "Yessir, Masta', sir." He backed out of the room, turned, and rushed outside to the kitchen to relay the master's orders.

Blackburn picked up the brandy decanter off a small table beside an upholstered chair and poured a generous quantity into the snifter. Replacing the crystal stopper, he picked up his glass and left the library. He turned right and through another door off the short passage, entering his bedroom. He removed his frock coat and draped it across a wooden straight-backed chair. Leaving his bedroom, he crossed into the great hall of his plantation house. It was a large room with high ceilings and two large wooden doors at the north and south entrances to the house. Wooden chairs and benches graced the hall to accommodate visitors as they awaited an audience with the owner of the plantation.

Blackburn crossed the hall and into another short passage. The door to his left led into the parlor. The one on the right led into the dining room. He passed over the threshold into the dining room. The Queen Anne table shone with a luster that Blackburn could have seen his reflection in had he cared to look. He pulled out a chair and sat down heavily. He stared blindly at his mother's delft china plate and did not hear the soft footfalls of Hattie and another slave as they carried the dishes to breakfront. A clatter of the dishes caused a small jerk to the hand holding the snifter.

"Pardon me, Masta'," Hattie said, as she cautiously picked up the china plate and removed it to the breakfront. She and the other Negro woman swiftly filled the plate with smoked trout, sausage, roasted potatoes, dried apples, and plums. Homer entered with a bottle of red wine and filled the crystal stemware three-quarters full. He stepped back beside the women and awaited his master's pleasure.

Blackburn began to eat as his mind churned over the last thirty-six hours. Now that he had time to think, reaction was setting in, and he thought about the consequences of his actions. He had made many errors of judgment. The bodies of the boy and slave would be found, and an inquiry would soon follow. Banister would not be well pleased at the demise of his trusted Negro. Blackburn's fingers clenched the stem of the wineglass in a tight grip as he thought of the lie he had told the farmer. If questioned by the authorities, the farmer could describe Blackburn and would repeat the untruth he told. How could he be so foolish! Banister would demand to know why he had claimed Ezra as his own Negro.

Blackburn eased his grip on the glass and took a sip of wine. He could persuade the authorities that the farmer was confused. Who would they believe a farmer, or a Burgess of the colony? He nodded his head and looked across the table as if an invisible guest had given him this sage bit of advice and not his own mind. As to the lass, he would question her carefully to find out if anyone would come seeking her or the lad. He relaxed further and sliced off a piece of sausage with his knife and raised it to his mouth. Chewing thoughtfully, he replayed the last conversation with the lad and slave. Did they indeed know of the jewels? Blackburn knew he would get no cooperation from the lass tonight. He would leave off with his questions until the morrow after he determined with his own eyes whether the jewels had been pilfered. Erasing the problems of the day from his mind, Blackburn belched into his monogrammed napkin before continuing his meal.

Em stared at the plate of food before her but could summon no desire to eat. She sat at a small table set before a large window that offered a view of the vast lawns of the estate. At the moment, the night sky hid the splendor of the early spring foliage. Em picked up her fork and pushed at a piece of apple. She felt hollowed out. As if all her crying had drained the fluids from her body. She turned to the dark pane and looked fixedly at the reflection of the flame as it danced atop the candle resting in the brass candlestick. Em's thoughts were at their bleakest. *Oh, Lord I can't do this, whatever this is. Not without Josh.* She bowed her head in abject misery.

Em's head snapped up at the feeling of invisible arms encircling her and the warmth that infused her body. Stunned, she thought. *God is...?* And then her thought was interrupted by a voice in her head. Three words: *He is alive.* Before she could blink the feeling left her. But she knew without question that God had spoken to her in her despair. A relief so profound, she could not explain it, filled her, and she trembled.

Em took a deep breath and looked at the plate of food. She picked up her fork and pierced two pieces of dried apple. She had to eat to keep up her strength. *Josh was alive.* With renewed determination, she continued to eat until every scrap was gone. Then she picked up the glass of wine. Her parents didn't drink alcohol and she knew she shouldn't either, but she had snuck a couple of sips of wine at her Aunt Katy's elaborate Christmas dinners. Em took a cautious sip and ran her tongue across her bottom lip. It wasn't bad, kind of fruity. But after only three sips, she set the glass on the table and pushed it away.

Placing her hands on the edge of the table, Em rose and resumed her pacing over the wooden floorboards. She barely registered the opulence of the room that held her prisoner. She did not see the rich colors of the cranberry and gold wallpaper or the head and footboards of the mahogany bed that had been ornately carved to match the dresser and wardrobe. She did not notice the beautiful black and beige wool rug that covered the wooden floor at the foot of the bed or the oil painting of the deceased mistress of the plantation hanging above the fireplace mantel. This room paid homage to a very wealthy woman. Em could have cared less; she was planning another escape attempt. The last one had failed miserably. Earlier when the key had turned in the lock, she had tensed her body, waiting for the right moment to run through the door.

Two black slaves had entered, a robust woman carrying her supper on a tray and a large man. The woman had hastened to the small table and removed the plate, napkin, flatware, and glass of wine from the tray, while the other slave stood in front of the door. He blocked the entire door, but his legs were spread far enough apart that Em figured she could duck through them before he realized her intentions.

Em dashed straight at the slave, and as he reached his arms out to grab her, she ducked and fell to her knees scrambling as fast as she could go through his legs. She might have laughed had she seen the stupefied look on Homer's face as she crawled through his legs. Homer reached between his legs and grasped a handful of Em's dress, dragging her back in front of his legs. With arms bulging with muscle, Homer grasped Em under her armpits and lifted her to her feet. Em started to struggle, but stopped at the anguished look on the slave's face. His eyes spoke volumes. *He doesn't like what Blackburn's doing anymore than I do.*

Realizing his hands were still on the young white woman, Homer quickly pulled them to his side and stepped back. His face took on a blank look as he stared at the floorboards. "Miz, I'm Homer. I can't be letting you leaves this room. Masta' Blackburn's orders."

No words came to Em as the black woman walked around Em and paused outside the doorway, laying the empty tray on a table Em could not see. When she turned back, she held a lit taper and proceeded to light candles and a chimney lamp around the room. Finished, she stepped past Homer and Em, disappearing down the hallway. Homer backed out of the room, his eyes warily watching Em as he shut the door behind him. Em winced when the key turned in the lock.

Without warning a furious anger had bubbled up and out through her mouth. "I hate this century! Can you hear me, *Masta'* Blackburn? This century sucks!"

Em had looked around for something to smash. A delicate figurine of a bird, displayed on the dresser, caught her eye. If its wings had been real, it would have flown away in a panic. Em walked over to the dresser and picked up the delicate knick-knack. But looking at it caused the anger to drain away and her tears flowed. Replacing the bird, she had walked to the table set with her meal and sat down.

Em stopped pacing. She stared at the locked door. She had tried earlier to pull the pins out of the hinges, but they were wedged too tight. Her eyes moved slowly over the surface of the door and then stopped on the lock. She smacked her forehead. *A key! She hadn't thought to look for a key.* Blackburn's mother would have a key inside the room to lock it for privacy. Blackburn had just shoved her in the room and locked the door with a key Homer had given him.

Em began a thorough search of every drawer in the room but could not find a key. She lifted the candle off the dresser and pursed her lips in concentration. She hadn't checked the dressing room. She crossed the room and looked inside. The only possible place for the key to be was a vanity table made of a darkly varnished wood. A cushioned chair sat between two drawers to the left and right. One drawer sat in the middle of the table six inches above the chair. Resting on top of the table were multiple small shelves and drawers with a swivel mirror in the middle. A few bottles of perfume and powders jostled for space on the polished surface. She set the candle down and searched each diminutive shelf and drawer carefully, but found only earrings, necklaces, and other costume jewelry of the era. Next she checked the two large drawers on either side of the cushioned seat. Nothing. Em sat down and opened the middle drawer, pulling out crystal jars of powders and others of pastelike consistency in various shades of red.

After emptying the middle drawer, she reached to the back and felt around. There wasn't a key, but she felt the bottom of the drawer dip down a fraction of an inch. Curious, she pressed down with the fingers of both hands. The back of the drawer sank a couple of inches, causing the front to pop up. Em carefully removed her fingers from the back and hooked them under the edge of the thin piece of wood, slowly raising it until she could move it toward her and remove it from the drawer. She laid it on her lap as she stared at the object in the drawer. *It couldn't be!*

CHAPTER 10

E m touched the soft leather. Another hidden diary. She looked up and smiled. *What were the odds?* Tentatively, she reached into the drawer and pulled out the slender book, turning the cover. On the inside was the name *Nessa Murray Blackburn.* Em turned the first page and started to read.

July 1, 1756

I purchased this handsome tome on our monthly trip to Norfolk. Ten years ago I could neither read nor write, but with the lessons every day from the Quaker Josiah Godfrey, I can now do both. Ewan does not know of my purchase. Not that he would disapprove. Ewan indulges me far more than I deserve. We have just now moved from the two-storied wooden home we lived in for the last ten years into this brick monstrosity Ewan had specially built for me and our new station in life as wealthy landowners. Rather he would not approve of putting our secret to paper. But I have a hiding place I am sure no one will discover. The guilt eats at me. I believe writing it down may ease that a bit. Where shall I begin? Well, at the beginning, I do suppose.

Our change from poverty to prosperity began in April 1746, not long after our Bonnie Prince Charlie was defeated at Culloden, on a clear day near our croft in the Hielands of Scotland. Ewan ran into our cottage out of breath. In his hand he clutched a black leather bag. He told me that the Laird was deid. He had been tending the sheep when he heard the pounding of horse hooves and Laird McLeod came thundering down the road riding his big gray horse. The horse had stumbled as one hoof landed in a large hole created by the recent rains. The laird had been thrown hitting his heid on one of the many rocks strewn across the pasture. Ewan had rushed over, but he could tell by the awkward angle of his heid and his eyes staring at nothing that he must be deid. A few feet from the laird lay a leather bag. Ewan picked it up and looked inside. Then he had rushed to the cottage to show me. I gasped at the sight of the many gems in the pouch: rubies, sapphires, diamonds, and emeralds. Ewan said to hide the pouch whilst he ran to the castle to inform the household of the death of the laird. I begged him to return the stones. If it was discovered that we had them, we would hang. But Ewan insisted that no one would know we had possession of the stones. He had a plan that he would reveal upon his return. I concealed the gems beneath the pallet on the bed frame and awaited Ewan.

Many hours passed and my anxiety grew. It was evening tide when he returned. He told me his plans whilst he supped. He could think of no one the laird would share knowledge of these gems with. His wife had died two years ago, and his only son had died at Culloden. Ewan said he had never seen any kin visit the laird. He was riding his gray hard as if he was fleeing. With the Stuart heir on the run, the British were likely to hang any sympathizers. And Laird McLeod would most certainly be arrested. The gems were most likely a bribe to hide him on a ship bound for France and for living expenses after he arrived. But surely someone knows of their existence? I said. Ewan repeated that he thought not, but said we would be long gone by the time suspicion would fall to him. But they are not ours, I said. Ewan's face grew dark, and he spoke with bitterness. How many times did wee Angus cry with hunger because the laird took the little food we had. Ewan was right.

Laird McLeod was not a fair master. I feel no guilt, he said. We would follow the same plan as the laird would execute and bribe passage to France. But who could we trust to help us? I asked. We knew nothing of bribery or ships or finding a home in France. That gave him pause. We do not speak the French tongue, he admitted. The English colonies in the Americas would be a better place to start anew. I was so frightened. Through the night we argued back and forth until exhaustion took us and we sought our slumber.

By supper the next day Ewan had mapped out our course. On the morrow he would go to my brother Stefan, in Inverness. He labored at the port unloading and loading goods on the ships. He may know which captains could be bribed. Ewan left before dawn the next day, and I clung to the door frame as he disappeared into the dark. I fed Angus and finished chores, awaiting Ewan's return at dusk. By the exhausted smile upon his face, I knew his journey was a successful one. For one of the larger stones, a captain, William Murphy, would grant us passage to Norfolk, Virginia, aboard the **Bonnie Lady.** *He would ask no questions about how we acquired the stones. As payment for his assistance, Stefan would accompany us. But we must bide our time until the weather favored a safe passage.*

In June, Ewan, meself, and four-year-old Angus stepped aboard ship. Stefan, alas, did not join us. The landlord at his bed and board informed us that Stefan had caught the ague and died within two days even as his body shook violently. I wept as Ewan consoled me as best he could. Ewan was right about the gems. No one came to the cottage to ask us about them, and there was never any whisper about their existence. Ewan believes that they were smuggled to the laird from France, but we will never know the truth of the gems. I had never been aboard a ship and was all atwitter. After we put out to sea, I stayed prone in my bed with a bucket near, my belly under the utmost distress. The motion of the seas did not seem to affect Ewan, and he spent most of the voyage caring for Angus or above helping the hands on deck. Ewan told me he had many a pleasant conversation with the captain at mealtimes. Captain

Murphy owns a sheep farm not too great a distance from Inverness. Ewan said he was vague when the captain inquired about his knowledge of sheep. Two days' distance from Norfolk, the captain gave Ewan the name of a certain person who could convert one of the gems to British coins. After docking and debarking, we followed the captain's directions

Em stopped reading as the pressure from her bladder became more insistent. She sighed in defeat. No matter how badly her mind did not want to use a chamber pot, her bladder didn't care. She rose from the chair and went on the hunt, eventually locating the disgusting thing under the bed. *Ridiculous, someone trying to pretty it up with green leaves and roses.* She carried it over to a corner. Having never used one before, she tried a tentative squat. Her long legs were a definite disadvantage. After a couple of attempts, she gave up. Why couldn't there be a potty chair, like the last century she visited. *Potty chair!* Glancing around, Em noticed a plain wooden chair. She carried the chamber pot across the room and placed it on the chair. Her eyes lit with pride, as if she had just invented the toilet.

Em placed the lid on the chamber pot and returned to the dressing room. She had just reached the vanity table when she heard the sound of the key turning in the lock. She shoved the book and piece of wood back in the drawer and shut it. Then she opened one of the jars of rouge and applied a little to her face at the sound of footfalls coming in her direction. She looked up as Homer paused in the doorway, a young female slave peering around his large physique.

Em spoke to the young girl, "What's your name?"

The girl did not answer.

"Lettie be deaf," Homer said. "You shouldn't ought to be touching the mistress's personal things."

Em rose from the chair and faced Homer. "Then let me out of this room and I won't be able to."

Homer took a step back at Em's tone. She brushed past him as Hattie bustled through the bedroom door with a tray and gathered up the empty plate and other supper items. She avoided eye contact with Em as she left the room.

"That be Hattie. She be fixing the food."

Em glanced at the large woman as she hurried away and then back to Homer.

"I be leaving an' locking the door whiles Lettie helps you to gits out of yo skirts an' such."

Em felt panic building. "No! I don't need help. I prefer to undress myself." Her eye caught sight of the chamber pot. "Could you empty the pot, though?"

Homer turned to Lettie and made a strange gesture with his hands. Lettie picked up the chamber pot and left the room. Homer stood mute until Lettie returned with the empty pot.

"We be back in the morn." Homer removed himself and turned the key in the lock.

Em stepped over to the thick quilt on the bed and sat down. That was close. No one could know she had nothing underneath her dress except her bra and panties.

Em walked slowly over to a gilded floor-length mirror that leaned against the wall and looked at her reflection by the glow of the chimney oil lamp on the nightstand next to the bed. She was a mess. Her hair was in frizzy disarray. The hem of her dress was stiff with mud. She reached into her pocket and pulled out the mobcap and a few bobby pins. She removed the neck scarf. She set the items on the dresser.

Em turned back to the mirror and ran a finger across the scar on her neck from cancer surgery two years before. Touching it helped to anchor her. She had begun to feel a lot like Alice after she fell down the rabbit hole and was even starting to doubt her sanity. But the scar was real. It reminded her of her family and the love and support they had showed her through the whole cancer ordeal. Em was no longer mad at her mother; instead she longed to climb back out of the rabbit hole and be held in her strong arms. Em heaved a sigh, turned from the mirror, went back to the dressing room, and removed the piece of wood and book.

After docking and debarking we followed the captain's directions to a tavern within easy walking of the wharf. All the buildings looked to be recently built. The captain told Ewan that Norfolk Borough had only been founded ten years before. Our only possessions were the gems placed in a pocket sewn to the underside of my skirts. Ewan inquired of the tavern keeper the name given him, and we were pointed to a man sitting alone at a corner table. Ewan told me and Angus to sit at a table occupied by three women and a baby whilst he conducted our business. He returned ten minutes later and told me to remove myself to the necessary and take a ruby out of the leather bag. The man left the tavern with the ruby, and I feared we would never see him again. Two hours later he returned with a large leather pouch. He handed it to Ewan, who perused the contents. Ewan removed a coin and made payment to the man for his service. The man gave a brief bow and returned to his corner table. Ewan hustled us from the tavern. We traveled a short distance to another tavern. Ewan inquired of lodging for a week and transportation to Williamsburg. He paid with a coin, and then we retired to our room.

Once the door was latched, I asked Ewan about the coins and our destination. Mister Treadwell would continue to convert our gems to coinage as needed as long as he remained honest about each transaction and he asked no questions. By the weight of the pouch, Ewan believed Mister Treadwell to have fetched a fair price. He dumped the contents of the pouch on the bed, and I gasped. Angus picked up a coin to examine it in his wee hand. There were so many of them, but at the time I knew nothing of their worth. Ewan had questioned Captain Murphy about British coins during our voyage. Excitedly, he pointed out guineas and sovereigns and such, but it meant nothing to me. Is Williamsburg to be our new home? I asked.

— SARAH NORKUS —

He was unsure. The galley cook aboard the ship had mentioned a visit he had made to Williamsburg. Ewan felt it would be a good place to start. I voiced my major concern. What if someone questions our departure from Scotland? Ewan put a gentle hand upon my shoulder and told me not to be concerned. Many people were fleeing Scotland after Culloden because of the fear of hanging. We would not receive a passing thought. Ewan hid the pouch under a loose floorboard, and we descended the staircase to supper.

The next day was spent inquiring as to the whereabouts of a seamstress. Ewan explained that our clothing needed to be of a nobler quality or suspicion would arise as we spent our coins. I felt quite the lady as I entered the inn in my fine garb a week later. Three of the regulars sat at one of the plank tables in close conversation. They turned, their curious eyes following our retreat up the stairs. We rose early in the morn to meet our transport. Ewan, Angus, and I traveled in a wagon with a gentleman delivering goods to Williamsburg. Our journey was long and arduous. There were no flat dirt roads, only ruts that jostle the body. Angus cried until he fell asleep. I became uncomfortable in my new finery and heaved a blessed sigh when I finally removed it in our room at the Raleigh Tavern in Williamsburg. For the next few days Angus and I walked the main street of Williamsburg and visited the various vendors' shops whilst Ewan talked with the businessmen of the town. I longed to purchase more items, but Ewan said we must wait. On our fourth day at the Tavern, Ewan strode into our room with a huge grin upon his face. He had befriended a gentleman who had agreed to petition to the governor for a hundred acre parcel of land on Ewan's behalf. As we awaited word, Ewan made several good contacts to help him gain knowledge about the running of a tobacco plantation. The petition was granted within a fortnight, and we packed supplies onto a cart for the trip to our new home in Dinwiddie County.

Our first glimpse did not fill me with delight, but neither did it fill me with despair. The fields were overgrown, gone to seed. The house needed painting and some repairs, but it

— 100 —

was two floors, and once inside I became enchanted with all the rooms. It was so different from our cramped one-room cottage. Instead of a dirt floor, it had a wooden floor! Ewan said the small dwelling behind the house was the kitchen. There were stables and wooden buildings for hanging tobacco. I had learned much about tobacco at our suppers at the tavern. The men seemed to talk of nothing else. This would be our main income, so suspicions would not arise and people would not become inquisitive about our status. Ewan had already put about a deception of an inheritance from an uncle. But he said we still must not arouse curiosity with opulent purchases. Ewan and the property agent shook hands as I began to unpack the cart. Ewan and I would make another trip to Norfolk to exchange gems for money, and I would shop for the essentials unavailable in Williamsburg.

Em paused in her reading of the entry as she considered going to bed. But she didn't think she could sleep, and she was now fascinated by Nessa's story. She was positive that this was what Blackburn was looking for at Battersea. But why there? Whatever jewels were left would have been hidden here. She turned another page and continued to read.

Once settled in our new home, I could not have been more content. Although reluctant, Ewan purchased slaves to work the fields. You needed many hands to harvest tobacco. He vowed to treat them with a decency not afforded us in Scotland. Angus, the wee little devil, would not leave the gems alone. No matter where Ewan hid them Angus managed to find them. A month does not go by that I do not discover him in one hiding place or another fascinated by their sparkle.

One day almost a year after our move to this new land, the gems went missing and Angus cried and swore he did not take them. Angus had turned six and begun to be sly. He would steal sweets from the kitchen right under Hattie's nose and deny it despite whippings by Ewan. Ewan whacked his behind good over the disappearance of the stones, but although he cried, he still refused to admit he did it. At supper the following night Ewan said he thought one of the slaves that helped with my chores in the house had stolen the gems. He would deal with the Negro on the morrow. Turning in my direction he winked. I watched Angus as a look of relief crossed his face followed closely by a crafty one. The next day I told Hattie to make up a cold fare for the noon meal as I would take it to Ewan in the south field. But instead of going to the field I hid myself and waited. Ewan was hiding in the stables. I heard the rear door to the house shut quietly and peered around a tree as Angus ran toward a thicket of trees at the edge of the property. He looked back a few times to see if he had been followed. Once he disappeared I ran for Ewan. I watched as Ewan circled around and came at the trees from a different direction. I stood frozen in the doorway of the stables listening. Ten minutes later father and son emerged. I could see the bag clutched in Ewan's hand. Instead of tears Angus looked angry and defiant. Ewan sent him to his room with nothing to fill his belly for the duration of the day.

At supper we discussed what to do. Ewan said he thought it would be best to hide the gems a distance from the plantation and convince Angus that he sold all of them. He wanted Angus to forget they ever existed. He said he knew the perfect hiding place quite a few miles west where he had been hunting deer. Only one more gem was needed for expenses to tide us over until the first tobacco crop was harvested. Then if another gem was required, he would use the tale of hunting deer to retrieve one. Ewan described the approximate miles, a bluff over a river, and other details so I would have knowledge of the gems' location should an accident befall him. I listened, although I do not think I could have found it.

Now Angus is a lad of fourteen, unruly, mean spirited, and spoiled. This is why the guilt eats at me. Had we not taken the gems and stayed in Scotland, would he be thus? I have had no more children. Was I cursed because of the gems? I shudder at the thought of where Angus would go and what he would do if he ever got his hands on the remaining jewels. I must be sure he never does.

Em turned the page and discovered that ten years had now gone by. She read the last entry.

April 1767

My heart is broken as I write this passage, and I have locked myself in my room. Ewan was struck by lightning at the midnight hour as he rushed to help remove the horses from the stable that had caught fire during the horrendous storm that ravaged our plantation a week ago. He was laid to rest three days ago and his will read today. Angus stormed from the solicitor's office in a fit of rage after discovering all of Ewan's assets had been left to me.

I am writing in this book again because of the coincidence. The day Ewan was killed he had returned from Williamsburg with the news that John Banister had just purchased the property where the remainder of the gems are hidden, and he planned to start building a home there soon. Ewan had planned to ride there on the morrow and retrieve them.

I will not retrieve them. Hopefully they will stay hidden forever and no one shall be tempted by their seductive sparkle. I feel the same as I did eleven years ago and will not tell Angus of the gems. He would gamble the worth away in a fortnight.

The gems were given to us by fate in April, and Ewan died in April. Fate is not kind. I should pray for my son's soul. But alas, I do not believe he has one. I believe I will die soon, for I have nothing to live for.

Em felt sad and numb with shock at the same time. *To watch your son change over time into an unfeeling, amoral caricature of a human being must have been heartbreaking.* A few minutes passed and the shock began to ebb. The gems *were* at Battersea, and

Blackburn thought she knew where. *But how did he find out?* Not from the diary. She was positive it had stayed hidden from the day Nessa first covered it with the thin piece of wood. Besides Blackburn wouldn't have returned it to the drawer after reading it; he would have destroyed it. Blackburn's mother might have caved on her deathbed. Maybe her son had been in some kind of financial difficultly and she felt guilty.

Em stared into the mirror without seeing her reflection. She was back on the cliff listening to Blackburn's furious rant about his secret legacy. He didn't just want to find the stones; he was *desperate* to find them. For the first time Em realized exactly how much trouble she was in. If he didn't find the gems, she needed a convincing lie to guarantee she was more valuable alive than dead.

Em carefully replaced everything exactly as she had found it. Rising from the vanity's chair, she crossed the threshold into the bedroom and strode to the dresser in search of something to wear to bed. She pulled out a long blouse smelling of lavender. Standing in front of the mirror, Em unzipped her dress and started to remove it when she noticed the dark window. With the light from the candles someone may be able to see her.

Em crossed back to the dressing room with the blouse and removed her dress and stockings. She had removed her shoes a few hours before. She stood undecided about her bra, but decided to leave it on. She slipped the blouse over her head and tugged it down as it was a bit snug. Em blew out candles as she crossed the room, goose bumps popping up on her body from the cold that had penetrated the room. She slipped shivering beneath the heavy quilt, leaving the chimney lamp lit. Her mind whirled with possibilities for the tale she would tell. Thirty minutes later, despite her fears for Josh and Ezra, utter exhaustion overcame her and she slept.

Chapter 11

J osh's limbs jerked convulsively as his body reacted to the
terror of the nightmare.

*He was running, running, trying to reach Blackburn before
he pulled the trigger. Em stood on the edge of the bluff, crying and
shouting "Josh, Josh" over and over. Josh yelled Em's name as he ran,
but Em could not hear him. As he closed the distance between himself
and Blackburn, Blackburn turned and looked at Josh. Time slowed
as Blackburn turned back to Em and pulled the trigger. "No!" Josh
skidded to a stop as he watched the ball from the pistol hit Em square
in the chest. For an eternity time stood still, and then Em pitched off
the cliff, her arms flailing and a scream torn from her throat. Josh
tried to race for the cliff, but it felt as if his feet sank down in mud
with each step as he strained every muscle in his body to get to Em.
He reached the edge, and his eyes did a desperate scan of the river
below. There was no ledge to catch her fall, and he knew she had been
swept away by the current. Grief and rage intermingled, and he
howled like a demented animal. He turned to seek revenge upon his
enemy. Blackburn fired the pistol again. Josh felt the ball penetrate his
stomach and he was falling, falling…*

"Josh, Josh! Cease struggling or you shall knock us both off
the ledge."

Josh's eyes snapped open, and he stared up at Ezra. The nightmare was fading, and his heartbeats slowed to their normal rhythm. "I was dreaming that Blackburn shot Em and she was dead."

Ezra's facial features were becoming defined as dawn broke across the river.

"Nay, Josh. Only tricks of the slumbering mind. I believe your Em to be well. Even if Master Blackburn has captured her and removed her to his home, he will not kill her."

Josh felt the damp chill of the early morning and started to shiver. Awkwardly, he pushed his sore body up into a sitting position, staring as the morning light backlit the woods on the opposite cliff. He was having a hard time coming to terms with events of the last two days. His shoulders slumped at the overwhelming sense of despair.

Ezra placed a gentle hand on Josh's shoulder. "Joshua, do not be despondent. We will find Miss Emily."

"Not if we can't get off this ledge."

Ezra looked out across the river as a ribbon of sun sliced around the trunks of the trees atop the neighboring bluff. He switched his gaze from the trees to the water rushing over the rocks toward the tranquil eddies a mile downstream. Ezra rose to his feet and stretched his arms over his head. He bent at the waist and removed his shoes. Next he unbuckled his stockings and shoved them into his shoes. He reached up to remove his straw hat, forgetting that it had fallen into the river the day before.

"Hey, man, how come you took off your shoes and...?"

Ezra swung his arms in an arc and leapt from the ledge. Josh stared in disbelief as he watched Ezra land with a huge splash equal distance between two large rocks. Josh scrambled to the edge, eyes straining for a glimpse of his friend. Ezra's head rose briefly above the surface of the river only to disappear again. Josh gripped the lip of the ledge, held his breath, and prayed. The breath came out in a whoosh as he spotted Ezra's head nearer to the bluff, but moving swiftly downriver. His last glimpse of Ezra was right before the bend in the river, arms pumping desperately for the riverbank.

Once he was gone from sight, Josh pushed himself back up against the cliff and whispered over and over. "Please, my man, make it." Josh slowly became aware that something was digging into his back. Madder than a wet hen at the situation in general and Ezra in particular, Josh turned and slammed his fist against the offending piece of the bluff. To his astonishment a piece of rock the size of his fist popped out. He picked it up turning it back and forth in his hand. He eyed the hole then slowly slid the rock back in place. It fit almost seamlessly. Josh pulled the rock out again and reached his fingers toward the hole. His hand stopped just short of the opening and then retreated. The picture of a large spider bloomed in his mind. Cautiously, Josh bent down and gazed into the opening.

The sun rising across the river gave enough light so that Josh could see something in the hole. Spiders forgotten he reached his hand into the opening. His fingers brushed across loose shale and then curled around something made of soft leather. Closing his hand around the object, he gently removed it from the gap in the rock face. It was a black leather bag with a leather drawstring. Josh loosened the drawstring and turning the bag over shook it above his open palm. Three large gems dropped onto the soft palm of his hand. A child's delight over a treasure found shone from Josh's eyes. He gazed with rapture at an oval emerald, a round ruby, and a square sapphire.

"Oh, man, oh, man...I can't believe...oh, sweet, sweet, sweet!"

Josh looked skyward and whooped at the top of his lungs. Then he turned and shouted down the river. "Ezra, get your loyal black behind back here pronto! We are rich, my man!"

Josh leaned back against the cliff, his fingers closing over the jewels. Ezra was on his way. He knew it in his gut. And then they would search for Em.

Ezra crouched on the riverbank, his chest rising and falling in great heaving breaths. Water dripped off his slender frame, forming puddles in the soft mud on the bank. He gazed at the serenely flowing waters and could not believe that he had almost died half a mile up the river. Ezra's breathing evened out, and he rose on trembling limbs. He took a tentative step, his bare foot leaving an impression in the oozing mud. Satisfied that his legs would hold his weight, Ezra made his slow way up the steep embankment and into the woods.

Ezra paused as he came to the point where the woods thinned out beside the bluff, his wet clothes plastered to his body. He needed to rescue Josh before his master arrived. He gazed nervously at the house and then relaxed when he didn't see his master's horse tied up next to the front steps of the villa. The day laborers did not concern him. Master Banister owned only five slaves, preferring to pay a daily rate for temporary work rather than pay the cost of buying many slaves and providing their daily needs for life. The laborers would not know he had gone missing and would have no reason to report his activities to Master Banister.

Ezra left the woods and hurried to the back of the house, rounding the corner to the entrance of the west wing. One of the laborers was leaving the entrance, and Ezra waited beside the steps with his head lowered until he passed by. Quickly, he climbed the three steps and crossed the length of the room. He bounded up more stairs into the attic above the room. Lying on the floor next to a large wooden box containing an auger, hammer, planes, chisels, drawknives, and other tools was a coil of rope. Ezra grabbed it, bounded back down the staircase, and rushed out the door. A sense of urgency spurred him into an all-out sprint for the section of cliff directly above the ledge where Josh waited. He skidded to a halt at the edge, loose dirt crumbling to the ledge below.

Josh barely registered the shower of dirt that fell on his head and shoulders. He was still mesmerized by the jewels glittering in his hand. He cocked his head to one side. Had someone shouted his name?

"Joshua!"

He looked up and then scrambled to his feet. Ezra was waving to him.

"Ezra, look what I found! We're rich, man!" Josh held up the gems so Ezra could get a good look.

But Ezra wasn't looking. He was lowering a rope. Josh dropped the stones back in the leather bag and pulled the drawstring tight. Half of it broke off in his hand as the rope dropped across his shoulder. Josh quickly curled up the bag and shoved it deep in his breeches pocket. He grasped the rope and looked up. Ezra had his hand up in a wait-a-minute gesture. He disappeared from sight.

Although it could not have been more than a minute, it felt like an eternity. When he returned, Josh could see Ezra shouting at him, but he couldn't make out the words. He shook his head. Ezra put his hands together and pantomimed climbing the rope. Josh nodded yes and reached up to grasp the rope just above his head. He paused. He felt like he was forgetting something. Ezra's shoes and stockings! He scooped them up, shoving them as far as they would go in his pockets. He took hold of the rope with both hands in a tight grip. He pulled on it as hard as he could to test the strength. Satisfied it would hold his weight and praying that Ezra knew how to tie a good knot, Josh started climbing. The rope went taut and dug into the side of the bluff. Josh's shoes kept slipping off the loose shale, so with no help from his legs, Josh depended solely on the muscles in his arms to do all the work.

Ten exhaustive minutes later, Josh's head rose above the lip of the cliff, and Ezra gripped him by the shoulders and dragged the rest of his body over the edge. The morning dew on the grass dampened his shirt and vest as Josh tried to catch his breath. He watched Ezra untie the rope from one of the pine trees and quickly coil it up. Saying that he would return swiftly, he raced for the house and rounded the corner. Josh had pushed to his feet when Ezra came rushing back. Indescribable emotions rose in Josh's chest and into his throat as Ezra drew near. Before Ezra could utter a word, Josh grabbed him in a hug so strong Ezra felt his ribs would crack.

"I will never forget this, Ezra. You risked your life to save me...and Em." He took a shaky breath and pushed back. "Ah, here are your shoes and stockings." Josh fumbled in his pockets, pulling them out and handing them to Ezra.

Ezra dropped to the ground and quickly pulled on his stockings and shoes. When he jumped back to his feet, Josh noticed a sheen of moisture in his eyes.

"Josh, I value you beyond my ability to articulate. You have shown me honor and respect and treat me as an equal. You are my fine friend. 'Tis something I do not take lightly. I will help you achieve your goal of returning to your time or die trying." Ezra grasped the upper part of Josh's blouse-clad right arm and squeezed it briefly.

"Now we must make haste before my master returns and detains us."

Together, the exhausted teens rushed to save a girl both knew that Josh could not live without.

Blackburn cursed loud enough that Homer and Hattie winced in fear as they laid out the dishes for breakfast on the sideboard in the dining room. Two pairs of eyes glanced at the wall clock making sure the cursing was not because they were serving breakfast past eight o'clock. The clock face showed fifty-five minutes past seven o'clock. But that gave neither cause to relax. Homer gazed uneasily through the doorway.

The door to Blackburn's bedroom banged open. Homer's uneasiness increased.

"Homer! Fetch my horse and a long length of rope to the front entrance."

Homer raced for the servants' entrance and the stables.

Blackburn cursed again as his boots stomped across the central hall and out the front entrance, pulling the door fiercely behind him. He was hours late to search Banister's property. He had consumed too much alcohol and overslept. Banister would no doubt be at the property by now. No choice, he would have to bluff his way through. He could not afford another delay. He slapped his riding crop against his right boot in aggravation as he hurried down the granite steps. He paused on the oyster shell circular drive impatiently awaiting the arrival of Homer.

Ten minutes later, Homer rounded the corner of the building, leading the stallion at a fast pace. Homer stopped abruptly as Blackburn strode toward him and jerked the coiled rope out of his hands and draped it across his chest and back. He stomped to the left flank of the horse to mount. He jerked on the reins, and the stallion snorted in protest, backing away. Blackburn jerked his head down.

"Be still, ye black heathen!"

The horse rolled his brown eyes and laid back his ears, but did as commanded. Blackburn turned to Homer.

"Do not let your guard down with the lass. She is as slippery as an eel. You will suffer greatly if she is not safely ensconced in my mother's room when I return."

Head bowed, Homer replied, "Yessir, Masta'."

Blackburn mounted and galloped off down the drive, the budding oaks lining the drive blurring as he passed.

Em started awake at the sound of loud cursing and a door slamming. Disoriented, she looked around the strange room. As comprehension dawned, Em hastily shoved the quilt aside and jumped from the bed, catching her foot in the dangling sheet and collapsing in a heap on the wooden floor. She shook her foot free, pushed hair out of her face, and then grabbed the elbow she had landed on. She winced with pain as the elbow throbbed. Grasping the side of the bed with her right hand, Em pulled herself upright. Another door slammed farther away.

Em pressed her ear up against the wood and strained to hear, but nothing came through. She slammed her fist against the door in frustration then yelped in pain. Now her hand and elbow hurt. Em sat down on the closest chair waiting for the pain to recede. She guessed that it had been Blackburn cussing and he had left the house to go look for the jewels, which meant... what? Two scenarios whirled in her brain. He found the jewels and killed her, or he didn't find the jewels and whipped her to make her confess where she and Josh had hidden them, and since she didn't know, she would probably die from the beating. Definitely a lose-lose situation. She had to escape. Em stared at the rectangular brass plate with the keyhole affixed to the door. Maybe she could manipulate the lock with something.

As Em started another search of the room, the key rattled in the lock. She swung back around as the door opened and Homer cautiously entered, scanning quickly behind the door and around the room. Em's lips curved in a wry smile. *He thinks I would hide behind the door and brain him with something heavy.*

Relief crossed Homer's face as he realized Em was too far away to try an escape. He opened the door wider for Hattie to enter with the tray of food. She quickly laid the contents on the small table and exited the room. Homer started to withdraw.

"Wait! No, don't go yet," Em pleaded.

Homer hesitated. "Miz, I'm…"

"Emily, my name is Emily. Please stay for a minute. I promise not to escape."

Em sent a quick prayer for forgiveness to God for the lie. She needed to keep him in the room as long as possible while she tried to think of something to get him away from the door.

"Your meal be waiting on you, Miz Emily."

Em sidled over to the small table. "I'll eat, just stay and talk with me for a minute."

Homer's brow furrowed in puzzlement as he stared at his worn shoes. "Talk, miz?"

"You know, uh…"—Em tried to think of another word for talk—"ah…converse."

"I knows what you means by talk, but whys you want to talks to the likes of me?"

"Careful," Em muttered to herself. She needed to remember what century she was in.

"What, Miz Emily?"

Em picked up her fork and knife and carved up a bit of venison. "How long have you been here?"

Homer scratched absently at a bug bite on his neck. "Well, I don't rightly knows."

Em grimaced as she chewed a piece of the cold venison. She tore a small chunk off the loaf of bread. "Do you know how to read and write?"

Homer's eyes grew big as saucers as he looked up and quickly back down. "Nay, Miz, I would be beat for being uppity."

"How long have you known Colonel Banister's slave, Ezra?"

Homer scratched more vigorously at the bite. "A long spell."

"But he reads and writes and is not beaten." Em picked up her fluted glass and took a big swallow. She barely managed to place the glass on the table as a coughing fit shook her body.

Homer looked up anxiously and took a step toward Em before remembering he should not touch the white woman and stopped dead in his tracks The coughing fit slowed, and Em took in a couple of big breaths. She glanced at the glass holding the pale brown liquid then turned her watery eyes up at Homer.

"What's in the glass?" she managed to squeak out.

"That be cider, Miz."

"What kind of cider?"

Puzzlement showed on Homer's face again. "Hard cider, Miz Emily."

At a visit to Pamplin Park, the adults had been able to sample hard cider, but it was too potent for children, and now Em knew why.

"That comes from a good barrel that been fermenting a season."

Oh, it had been fermenting all right, no doubt about it.

"Do you have any spring water?"

Homer was horrified. "What you wanting water for? That's just for the horses, slaves an' like."

Em rolled her eyes. *There I go thinking twenty-first century again.* But she couldn't keep drinking the cider, wine, and beer. She'd get so drunk she probably wouldn't notice if Blackburn did kill her. It occurred to her that she hadn't had anything to drink since yesterday afternoon, and she couldn't afford to get dehydrated.

"I know you're confused, but I need a big cup of water, Homer."

Homer hesitated for a moment and then replied, "Yea, Miz Emily."

Turning on his heel, Homer left to do Em's bidding, locking the door behind him.

Em took another cautious sip of the cider. An involuntary shudder came over her body. *Nasty stuff.* Em put down the glass and picked up her fork, continuing to eat the venison that sat in a small pool of congealed fat and spices. As she chewed, her mind whirled with escape possibilities. Finished with her meal, Em put down her fork. Homer was too strong. She was never going to force her way out. The key turned in the lock, and Homer entered with a blue tinted tumbler brimming with water. Em snatched it up as soon as Homer set it on the table. Swallowing as fast as possible, she relished the cold liquid.

Astonishment got the better of Homer, and he forgot to drop his eyes to the floor in deference as he watched Em gulp down the water like one of the stable dogs. Setting down the empty glass, Em let out an involuntary burp.

"Not quite a high fiver, but it will do," Em said as she raised her right hand toward Homer.

If Homer thought he could not be more astonished than he already was, he was wrong. His jaw dropped, and his mouth popped open.

Em couldn't stop herself from giggling. "My mom used to say, 'You better close your mouth before a hummingbird uses it for a nest.'"

Homer shut his mouth so fast his teeth clicked together. This white woman was not acting like any white woman he had ever served. All white folks made him nervous, but this one made him 'specially uneasy with her strange talk and ways.

"That be all, Miz Emily? I got to finish my chores afor the masta' returns."

Unable to come up with anything to detain him, Em sighed in frustration. Homer picked up the empty plate, cup, and utensils on his way to the door. Em set her elbows down on the table, balled her hands into fists, and laid her forehead on them.

CHAPTER 12

Josh and Ezra's shoes barely made a sound on the damp earth as they slowly jogged down the road toward Blackburn's plantation. They had argued briefly at the corner of Banister's property and the road. Ezra wanted to travel through the woods and the cover it afforded, Josh wanted to stick to what passed for a road in this century, which would get him to Em faster. Ezra deferred to Josh, and the teens took off at a dead run. Now two hours later, and near exhaustion, they had reduced their speed considerably.

Both boys were visibly anxious as they scanned the road ahead for any sign of Blackburn. They had both assumed that at some point they would have to duck in the woods to avoid Blackburn on his way to Banister's property to search for his treasure. But he had yet to appear, and that worried them. They figured he would want to search and be gone before Banister arrived.

Chest heaving, Josh asked for the third time, "Do you think he's done something to Em? We should have passed him by now."

Ezra stopped and dropped to the road, planting his face hard against the dirt.

"Ezra, dude, what are you doing?"

Ezra raised his hand and shook it for silence. A few seconds later he rose to his feet. "A horse is coming. I can feel the pounding of the hooves on the road. Hasten for the woods, Josh."

The boys scrambled across a small ditch and into the cover of the trees, dropping to their bellies behind some brush. Josh pushed aside a small portion of the vegetation and watched the road. A minute later, a black horse and rider flew by, dirt flying behind the horse's hooves. As the pounding faded, Ezra and Josh climbed to their feet.

"Master Blackburn, Josh?"

"He rode by too fast, I couldn't tell."

Ezra crossed over the ditch. "We must pray that Master Blackburn is not too soon finding his cache."

"No worries there, Ezra." Josh reached in his pocket and pulled out the black leather bag with the broken string. He opened it and poured out the three large jewels. As he looked for Ezra's reaction, he thought, *If his eyes bulge out any further, they're going to pop out.*

"Master Joshua! Pardon, Josh. Where did you acquire those gems?"

"It's Blackburn's treasure. I found it in a hole in the cliff while you were doing your *Indiana Jones* routine."

"Indiana...?"

"Never mind. The good news is we have what he wants. If we can't free Em on our own, we have a bargaining chip."

Returning the jewels to the bag, Josh shoved it into his breeches and started running down the road again.

Ezra kept pace beside him. "Josh, I should be heartily alarmed that we hold Blackburn's cache, but strangely, I am not. Indeed, I am exhilarated. Such a feeling that I have never felt before."

Josh smiled over at Ezra. "That is the feeling of freedom, my friend."

Blackburn slowed his horse to a trot as he approached Banister's villa. He turned onto the muddy track and slowed to a walk. A few laborers walked about the property, but there was no horse tied to the hitching post. Climbing down he looped the reins over the post. He hailed a laborer approaching the west wing.

"Is Mister Banister about?"

The laborer removed his straw hat. "Good day to you, sir. Begging your pardon, sir, I have not seen the good gentleman."

Blackburn sighed with relief, ignoring the man as he bowed. He climbed the steps and into the foyer. He crossed into the salon and out the back door. He strode quickly toward the bluff hoping to avoid a hail by Fletcher, who most assuredly was bound to be about somewhere. Arriving at the edge of the bluff, he thought about his mother's words. *Your father said there was a ledge. Only one, protruding from the cliff face.* He looked down and to his left, but saw no ledge. He turned to the right and there it was, a few yards to the right and a few feet down. The triumphant glee that flooded his brain quickly subsided as he realized the ledge was exactly below the spot where he had shot the boy. Blackburn tensed as his mind denied his body's reaction. *Not possible. If he had landed on the ledge, he would still be there.*

Blackburn relaxed when he saw no signs of blood. He would have been bleeding from the gunshot wound. He must have fallen past the ledge and into the river. Blackburn removed the rope from his body and strode to the closet tree to the cliffs, tying the rope to the same tree Ezra had used a few hours before. Hand over hand he carefully descended until his boots rested on the ledge. Now he had to find the loose rock affixed on the cliff face. Blackburn rubbed his hand along the rough surface of the cliff. Five minutes later, he located the rock. His fingers shook with anticipation as he pulled out the rock. He reached his hand into the hole and moved his fingers back and forth. *Empty!* His mind screamed the word, but he refused to believe it. He lay on his stomach to peer into the hole as his fingers desperately searched.

Stunned disbelief contorted his features as he pulled his hand out and absently wiped it on his frock. Starting to push up on his hands, he paused as something got his eye. His brow furrowed in puzzlement at the piece of frayed leather thong. He picked it up between thumb and forefinger. It was a drawstring to a leather pouch. Understanding dawned as Blackburn scrambled to a seated position. His anger slowly burned as Blackburn realized someone had found his legacy. Those interfering whelps!

Blackburn snatched the rope and climbed it as fast as possible. He rose to his feet on the edge of the bluff seething. As he stared at the raging water, an icy chill replaced his burning anger. What if the boy or the Negro had secreted the pouch in their breeches and the bodies was never found? Or someone discovered the bodies downriver and discovered the gems? Blackburn's fist clenched in rage. *The lass must know.* And he knew how to get the truth out of her. Untying and rewinding the rope, Blackburn turned and strode with a deadly calm back to his horse.

Homer sat in a wooden chair at the rough hewed wooden table in the cook house behind the main house. His mahogany face shone with sweat from the heat radiating from the flaming coals in the immense fireplace. He lifted a cracked crockery cup to his lips and swallowed some of the hard cider. Hattie placed a plate of cornpone in front of him, but Homer ignored it.

"Now, Homer, why's you not eating my fine batch of cornpone?"

Homer gave no answer.

Hattie planted her fists on her ample hips and glared at Homer. "Homer! What's wrong with you?"

"Ain't right, Masta' locking up Miz Emily."

"That's white folks' business."

"But I'm afeared for her. I'm thinking that Masta means to harm her. Maybe never lets her go." Homer's misery showed on his face.

Hattie came around the table and laid a hand on Homer's shoulder. "Now what makes you go believing such a thing. He ain't never harmed any of those women he brung here."

Homer lifted his eyes to Hattie's', causing her to look down at her apron in shame. "Not harm them? You knows he done took their virtue, Hattie. They was scared an' weeping when the Masta was done with them."

"I knows that, but there ain't nothing we can do. We let that girl go and we be beats near to death." Hattie strode back to the fireplace and the meal she was preparing.

Stomach churning, Homer pushed himself away from the table. He was afraid if he ate, he would be sick to his stomach. He walked through the doorway and out into the noonday sun. If his heart weren't so heavy, he would have appreciated the warm day and the buds opening on the flowering trees that covered the property. Flowering trees in the springtime had been a passion of his late mistress, and she had planted many around the plantation. He missed the mistress sorely. She had been as kind as the day was long. Her son was as mean as a copperhead you came upon unaware.

Striding toward the stables to make sure all was in readiness for his master's return, Homer noticed a slight movement at the edge of the wooded area off to his right. He turned his gaze in that direction but didn't see anything unusual. It was probably just a deer. Homer started to turn back when he saw it again. He couldn't be sure because of the distance, but it looked like the raised arm of a Negro man. Afraid something was wrong with one of the field slaves, Homer decided to investigate and strode quickly to the woods.

The woods were cooler, the sun-dappled leaves casting shadows on the patches of moss and emerging spring weeds. Homer cast his eyes around and saw movement to the left, behind one of the maples.

"Who's there?" Homer said.

Ezra moved from behind the trunk of the tree. "Good morn to you, Homer."

"What's you be doing here?" Homer's tone expressed his confusion at the sudden appearance of Master Banister's slave.

"We need your assistance, Homer. 'Tis a very grave matter…" Ezra paused. "For my friend."

Josh stepped from behind another tree. "Ezra means me. My name is Josh. It's nice to meet you." Manners ingrained since birth, Josh walked toward Homer with his outstretched hand.

Homer backed up as his confusion deepened.

Ezra shook his head at Josh, who stopped midstride, lowered his hand, and mumbled, "Stupid move."

"Homer, is your master detaining a lass, Miss Emily, against her will?"

Homer's eyes widened, but he remained silent.

"She is promised to Josh, and Master Blackburn has stolen her. He means her serious harm."

Homer took another step back in shock. Ezra could tell that Homer was as skittish as a colt ready to bolt.

"The tale is long, and your master will soon be returning. Please inform us, Homer, is she within the house?"

Homer knew if he said the girl was here and he helped them leave with the girl, he would most likely be lashed until he died.

Homer shook his head. "Nay, Ezra."

Josh started to say something, but Ezra shook his head.

Curiosity got the better of Homer, and he said, "Why's that white boy acting likes you is his masta'?"

"He has traveled a long distance and does not know our ways. Where he lives the Negro man is his equal, not a slave. I have agreed to assist with his cause and save his fiancé."

Homer's eyes widened again. "There be a place where the Negro is free an' equal with the white folks?"

Inspiration hit Ezra. "Yea, Homer, I am traveling there as soon as Miss Emily is reunited with Josh. You can travel with me. I am bound for freedom's road."

Homer's voice shook as he whispered, "You talking likes a runaway."

"Because of circumstances that have unfolded in the last two days, I cannot return to my master. But even if that were possible, I do not wish to. Josh has told me many tales about freedom as we journeyed here, and I will fight for such a life."

"That be crazy talk, Ezra!"

Josh had to voice the desperation he was feeling. "Please, Homer, is Emily here? I have to know!"

Homer could see the wetness in the white boy's eyes, which brought to mind the tears that had coursed down his cheeks when his own woman and girl-child had been sold off by Masta' Blackburn. He would never see them again.

Homer blurted the truth. "Miz Emily is here. But I don't wants to be killed or a runaway."

Josh's relief was so profound he steadied himself against the nearest tree so he wouldn't fall to the ground. Ezra helped to bolster him with a squeeze to his shoulder.

"Reveal to us where your master has detained her and we assure you that you shall not be accused," Ezra said.

Homer dropped his head and ran a large brown hand across his face. "I'm scarit, Ezra."

"I know, Homer, but think of your late mistress. You told me of her great kindness to you. What would she have you do?"

Homer's raised his head. "Let that poor child go."

There was the sound of thundering hooves off in the distant.

"That be my masta'. You stay hidden. I will return when it be safe." He raced for the stables.

"What? No wait!" Josh yelled.

Josh turned to Ezra. "No way, man, I'm not hanging around here. Blackburn could hurt Em!"

Before Josh could take a step, Ezra grasped Josh's arm in an iron grip.

"Josh, we cannot attempt a rescue of Miss Emily in broad daylight. We are not armed, and Master Blackburn most assuredly is. Nor do we know the layout of the house, and where Miss Emily is being held. We will bide our time and plan how to obtain her release."

It didn't matter that Josh knew Ezra was right. His instinct was to bust into that mansion and get her out now.

"Ezra, I have to go now. Blackburn must be furious because his jewels are gone—he might kill her!"

"He will not kill her. Master Blackburn will believe that we stole them and that Miss Emily knows the location of his cache."

Ezra's reasonable words penetrated into the small part of Josh's mind not consumed with fear but were quickly squashed. "But he will interrogate her, and she can't tell him where they are, so he will try to beat it out of her. I won't let him do that!" Josh's hands clenched into fists.

Ezra tried to be the voice of reason again. "Josh, Miss Emily is most capable of fooling Master Blackburn. Assuredly, she will confess to the whereabouts of the gems to buy time. And Homer's master cannot return to Master Banister's property until dawn on the morrow. We will obtain her release by then."

Ezra prayed to the God above that Josh would accept his words. He had almost died once by acting rashly.

Josh could almost feel his heart being torn in two pieces as he wrestled with the two choices. Which was the right one? To go now or wait? His terror was so great he could feel his nails digging into his palms.

"Josh, we must conceal ourselves." They could be seen when Blackburn left the stables.

Ezra melted back into the cover of the trees. Josh wiped the moisture from his eyes with the sleeve of his grimy blouse and turned back into the woods.

Homer's heart pounded in his ears as he slowed to a stop at the stable doors. He had no time to think about the situation that had been thrust upon him. His master's horse came to a halt bares inches in front of him, sides heaving and foam flying from his mouth as he shook his massive head. Homer grabbed the bridle as his master dismounted.

"Homer, fetch the key to my mother's room!" Blackburn demanded.

One of the stable lads rushed over and grabbed the bridle.

"Yea, Masta'," Homer said as he sprinted for the house.

As Homer descended the steps to the servant's entrance, he knew the sweat pouring off his face was not due to heat. He was so scared the spit had dried up in his mouth. Once in the butler's pantry just off the dining room, Homer opened the door to a small cupboard attached to the wall. Various keys hung upon wooden pegs. As he selected one, he heard his master's footfalls on the floor planks as he crossed the threshold of the back entrance. He quickly seized a serving towel and mopped all traces of sweat from his face. Homer took a deep breath and joined his master in the hallway.

Blackburn jerked the key from his hand.

"Come with me."

Homer followed Blackburn into the passage of the bedroom suites. Stopping in front of his mother's carved mahogany door, Blackburn slipped the key into the lock. As he started to turn the key, there was a loud knock on the front entrance door.

"What the devil!" Blackburn growled.

Homer rushed to answer the door. A gentleman, exquisitely attired, stood on the stoop.

"Mister Wolcott to discuss business with Mister Blackburn," the gentleman intoned.

Homer opened the door wider and indicated that the gentleman have a seat on one of the many benches along the walls. He returned to his master, who still stood in front of his mother's door.

"Mista' Wolcott, Masta."

"Blast and damnation!"

Blackburn shoved the key into his pocket. "Show the gentleman into the library."

As Blackburn strode across the passage, Homer hurried to the gentleman and led him to the library. After Mister Wolcott crossed the threshold, Homer discreetly closed the door. He stood in the passage and stared at the door that concealed Miss Emily. He needed to tell her about Ezra and that strange white boy. But he was so afeared he was starting to feel a sickness in his belly. He didn't know how long the masta' would be with the gentleman, and he needed a reason to be in the mistress' room if the masta' caught him there. Suddenly the reason came to mind, and Homer hurried to the butler's pantry and the extra key that had been removed from the mistress's vanity. With the key squeezed within his fist, Homer rushed to the cook house.

Moments later he returned to the house and crept on silent feet to his late mistress's door. As he inserted the key, he heard the latch lift on the door behind. He snatched the key back and shoved it in his breeches pockets as the door behind him opened.

Pleasantries accomplished and with small glasses of sherry in hand, Blackburn and Wolcott seated themselves in upholstered chairs across from each other.

"Now, sir, to what do I owe this pleasure?" Blackburn stated.

"I had business in the area to attend to and hoped to kill two birds with one stone, so to speak," Wolcott said as he absently fingered the end of the horse's whip that lay across his lap.

"Did you forget, Angus, that we were to meet at the King's Arm Tavern yesterday at noon?"

With a strong will, Blackburn stilled the slight trembling of his right hand. "No, Wolcott, I did not forget. I need but a few days more to acquire the funds to cancel the debt I owe you."

"Patience is a virtue, but I fear I am fast losing mine where you are concerned." Wolcott set his sherry down on the small table next to him and rose to his feet.

"If the five hundred pounds you owe me is not paid by noon one week hence, I will go to my barrister and have a lien placed against your personal property."

"There is no need to see me out. Good day to you, sir." Without a backward glance, Wolcott opened the door and strode from the library.

Blackburn watched him leave as the fury built within him. He pushed to his feet and downed the sherry in one gulp. He walked toward Homer, who was frozen as stiff as a statue with a pewter cup in his hand.

Ignoring Homer, Blackburn removed the key from his pocket. "That twit better know where my gems are or she will rue the day she came upon this world."

Inserting the key, Blackburn turned it, pressed down on the latch, and swung the door wide.

CHAPTER 13

The door banged against the wall, and Em jumped and spun around. Blackburn's face was so infused with blood it looked like it would burst if pricked with a needle. Fingers shaking, she pushed a stray lock of auburn hair behind her ear. She had heard Blackburn cursing through the door earlier, and dread had dropped like a rock in her stomach. Her search had become frantic. But there was nothing to be found. No key and no implement that could trip the lock anywhere in the room. By the look on Blackburn's face it was "game over." Her lies had better be beyond convincing. *Lord, please, please, give me strength.*

"You, lass, will play me the fool no longer! Where are my jewels?"

"I don't..."

Blackburn took two strides and snatched up Em's arm. Twisting it cruelly, he brought it up behind her back. Em yelped in pain.

"No more lies!"

"Okay, okay, let go of my arm!"

Blackburn let go and shoved her into a chair. Em cradled her arm and gritted her teeth against the burning in her shoulder. She spat out the lie she had prepared.

"The pouch with the jewels is in the wing of the villa where you were with Martha." Em paused. "In the gap in the floor."

"'Tis an untruth! You would not conceal them somewhere you could not retrieve them. The floor planks were placed over the gap two days ago."

"What?" Em stammered in shock.

Blackburn raised his arm, and Em knew he meant to slap her. Suddenly her fear disappeared and she was furious. No one had ever abused her!

"Hit me and I will *never* tell you where they are!" she screamed.

Blackburn dropped his hand. Something had changed. He could see no fear in her eyes. She was an enigma to him, not displaying the normal female traits he was accustomed to seeing in women. His thoughts swirled around his brain in desperation. *Threatening her was no longer going to give him the information he required. How was he going to get her to comply? He had to have those gems, or he would lose his plantation.*

Suddenly, he knew. *The lad. She would sacrifice her life for him.* A small falsehood would get him what he desired.

"I believe you will reveal the location if you wish to be united with your bonny lad."

Em's face paled. "What…?"

"I saw where he lay after his fall from the bluff."

Em's whole body trembled. "Is he…dead?"

Blackburn found himself quite satisfied with her fear but knew he had to give her a glimmer of hope to get back the jewels.

"When I descended to the ledge to recover the gems, I observed him moving his head on the riverbank below. You shall discover the seriousness of his injuries once the jewels are in my possession."

"We have to leave now! He could be dying!" Em scrambled out of the chair.

Blackburn grabbed both of her shoulders and pushed her back into the chair.

"Tell me the location of the gems and I will let you go to your beloved!" Blackburn insisted.

Em's anger returned. "Do you think I'm stupid? I'm not telling you anything until I see Josh!"

The blood returned to Blackburn's face, and only the realization that if he throttled her, he would never get the jewels kept Blackburn's hands at his side. His desperation was so great he wished to seize her, throw her across his horse, and gallop to the villa now. But the laborers would not leave till almost sunset, and he could not risk the lass screaming for help.

The fists that Blackburn clenched at his sides were white. "We shall depart before dawn. Do not attempt to trick Homer and escape, or I shall shoot yon fool again before you reach him."

"No! No! Now!"

Blackburn ignored Em as he passed Homer, still frozen before the threshold.

"Lock her in!"

Hastily, Homer set the pewter cup down on the closest surface and left the room, locking the door behind him.

Em leapt to her feet and pounded on the stout wooden door. "Come back! We have to go now!"

Em pounded and shouted for the next fifteen minutes, but it was futile. She lowered her throbbing fist and dropped to the floor sobbing. Gradually her weeping slowed and then stopped with two hiccups. She ran her sleeve under her running nose and took a deep breath.

Em rose to her feet and looked first at the damp spot on her sleeve and then down at her mud-caked hem. This was no longer the pretty dress she had pulled over her head a couple of days ago. She sat back down and tried to loosen the worst of the caked mud. As chunks of dried mud fell to the floor, Em's gaze caught her stockinged feet. Em pulled the stocking down on her left leg and over her foot to examine the blister. She unwrapped the strip of cloth Rebecca had wrapped around her foot. The salve had worked. The blister had dried up and was no longer painful. It was ironic. Em realized that she owed Blackburn for the fast healing since she had not needed to wear her shoes.

Absentmindedly, Em drew her stocking back up and over the lean muscle of her calf. *Where were her shoes?* Searching the bedroom, she finally located them under the bed. She slipped them on and walked the length of the bedroom to see if the shoe rubbed.

She sighed with relief. They felt fine. Pausing by the vast window, Em wrestled with the dilemma that faced her tomorrow. She had to fool Blackburn completely on the hiding place of the nonexistent jewels. But it had to be somewhere he could physically get to and she could not; otherwise, he would point the gun directly at her and tell her to bring the pouch to him. She just needed to think like a guy. Where would Josh have hidden the jewels?

Em stared out over the lawn surrounded by fields of tobacco and woods. Her gaze lingered on the woods, and a calm that could only be from God settled over her. Her hand reached out of its own accord, and she laid her palm gently against the pebbled pane of glass.

———◦◉◦———

Josh pushed the button on the side of his watch for the third time since darkness had enveloped the shadows beneath the trees. He noted the time in the watch's eerily blue glow.

"Ten o'clock! Why is it taking so long?" Josh whispered.

Ezra shifted his shoulders against the bark of the pin oak tree as he stared with the wonder of a young child at the timepiece on Josh's wrist.

"How is the light captured in the face of your timepiece?"
Ezra whispered back.

Josh paused before answering. "I'm not sure. I guess I'm not that curious about the inner workings of my electronics.

"Where is Homer?" Josh repeated anxiously.

"He must wait until his master has retired and would be asleep." Ezra leaned forward, wrapping his arms around his shins. "Pardon, Josh, but would you tell me more of this war that is coming."

Josh sighed. "Well, if you are going to Boston, you will be smack dab in the middle of it, my man. And what I'm going to tell you is just what I've been taught in school and I may not have all the facts right...but I believe the Boston Tea Party was the beginning."

Ezra raised an eyebrow, which Josh could not see in the dark. "A tea party? Why should grown men fight at a lady's tea party?"

Josh laughed, and then looked around guiltily. "It wasn't that kind of party. The taxes got so bad on the tea, the rebels dressed up as Indians and boarded a British ship, dumping all the tea over the sides."

"These men must have been quite perturbed, Josh."

"Oh, yeah, they were totally ticked. The British had also massacred a bunch of citizens. Anyway, the protests escalated, and the British called in their frigates to block the ports. The leaders of the rebels, like Samuel Adams, John Hancock, and Paul Revere, rode all over the place telling the colonists to take up arms and fight for their liberty. I think they were called the Sons of Liberty."

Ezra murmured, "The Sons of Liberty. Do you think they would allow a slave to join their cause?"

"If I remember right, quite a few black, ah, Negroes joined the rebels. But it's not something I would just jump into. You would be an enemy of the British, and it could be turn out the lights, the party's over for you," Josh said somberly. "And what about your master, Mister Banister? It's still five years until the revolution. Won't he find you?"

"I shall acquire a surname and pass as a freed Negro. I understand Boston to be a large place and quite a distance. My master will not search for me there."

"What will your last name be?" Josh asked.

"What is your last name, Josh?"

"Winters, but it's wrong for this time period."

Ezra was silent for a few minutes, and then he spoke, "In the Bible, Moses helped to set his people free. I shall be Ezra Moses. And I shall join the Sons of Liberty and help to free the Negro people."

"Sorry, Ezra, but the Negro people aren't freed until the Civil War in 1865. The north, like Boston, wanted to end slavery, and the south, like Petersburg, didn't. There were a bunch of battles, but after a few years the north won and the president, Abraham Lincoln, freed all the slaves. And I, uh, don't think Moses works as a last name."

Ezra was silent as he contemplated Josh's words.

"Ezra?" Josh said.

"This Abraham Lincoln freed the slaves? Then my new name shall be Ezra Lincoln." His voice grew strong. "And I shall fight with the white men of Boston for their freedom because a hundred years later, those fine gentlemen shall fight to end slavery."

Ezra gripped Josh's arm tight. "And I will gain my freedom."

Josh's voice was wistful. "I just wish I could know how your life turned out after I go back to my time."

After a few minutes, Ezra broke the silence. "I shall find a way. What month and year was it when you left?

"April 2009."

Josh could hear the awe in Ezra's voice.

"2009, I…" Ezra jumped to his feet instantly alert.

The sounds of soft footsteps were coming toward them. Josh rose cautiously to his feet as Homer called out in a low voice.

"Ezra, where you be?"

Ezra moved forward.

"The master be abed and the rest of the slaves be in their quarters. I brought you some cornpone."

Ezra accepted the cornpone wrapped in a muslin rag. Opening the rag, he held it toward Josh. Josh shook his head.

"What about Em?" Josh said.

"Miz' Emily be fine, sir."

Josh heaved a sigh of relief and felt the tension leave his body. "Let's go."

"Josh, eat first. It has been more than a day since we broke our fast. And we have yet to travel back to Master Banister's property."

Josh knew Ezra was right. His stomach had started to growl at the sight of the food. He grabbed two of the cornbread sticks and chewed as fast as possible.

Homer cleared his throat. "I don't knows as I can help, Ezra. I'm so afeared."

"Josh has thought of a plan so you will not be accused on the morrow," Ezra said around a mouthful of cornpone.

Josh's throat expanded as he swallowed. "Do you have the key to the room Em is in? Will the key make a lot of noise when you turn it in the lock?"

Homer pulled the key out of his breeches pocket. "I done greased up the door locks the other day."

Josh wiped his mouth with the back of his hand then wiped his greasy fingers on his breeches. "Okay, here's the plan. I go in the room first and put my hand over Em's mouth so she doesn't scream when I wake her. While she gets dressed, Ezra is going to strip the bed and tie the sheets together."

Josh paused. "Wait, I forgot something. Do the windows in the room open?"

"Yea, Lettie be opening the window for the mistress sometimes."

"Homer, you open a window while Ezra ties the sheets. Then we hang the sheets out the window to make it look like Em escaped. Then we leave the room and lock the door. In and out, and you won't be blamed."

"The masta's bid me sleep on the floor in fronts of the mistress's door. Masta Blackburn is gonna be in a mighty rage 'causes I not hear Miss Emily leaving out the window." Homer's voice quivered.

Ezra put a hand on Homer's arm. "You can travel with me to Boston, Homer."

Josh gripped Homer's other arm. "There are white men in Boston who hate slavery. They will hide you and fake papers to say you are a free Negro. Your master won't find you there."

"I'm to afeared to travel so far, and this be my home."

Josh gripped Homer's arm harder. "Please, Homer, I love her."

The image of his sweet baby girl came into Homer's mind. Still afraid himself, he slowly nodded his head.

The two teens left the woods close on the heels of Homer. The moon was three-quarters full and bathed their path with a dim light as they stepped onto the lawn of the estate.

Once they reached the rear of the house, Homer slowed and then stopped at the servants' entrance. All three looked around and then moved stealthily down the stone steps to the wooden door. Homer led them through a large storage area of barrels, casks, and numerous dried staples. A quick climb up another flight of stairs and they were in the butler's pantry.

Homer whispered, "There be some squeaking floorboards. Best to takes off your shoes and follow close."

All three removed their shoes. Homer opened the door, and the boys followed. On silent feet, Josh and Ezra followed Homer through the dining room and into a cavernous central hall lit by the stub of a candle with multiple layers of wax coating its brass candlestick.

Josh tried not to breathe as his heart pounded in his chest. Every nerve ending in his body was on high alert, and he vowed to himself that if Blackburn discovered them, he would not get the better of him this time. He trod close on Homer's heels as the black man avoided suspect floorboards. Homer crossed the hall into a short hallway and paused beside a dark carved door. He pointed down the hall at another door, and Josh understood that to be Blackburn's bedroom. He watched Homer slip the key in the lock, and although he would have thought it impossible, his heart beat even harder.

CHAPTER 14

Em lay on top of the bed fully clothed. She had decided on the well as the ideal place for the jewels to be hidden. She remembered hearing Colonel John Banister and Mister Fletcher talking about progress halting on the digging of a well, and she had noticed a large hole in the ground when she went to the privy. The only thing she didn't know was how deep the hole was. It had to be deep enough so that Blackburn would need a rope. She closed her eyes and sent a quick prayer heavenward that the well would be deep enough.

Em slowly sat up on the bed. *Had she heard something?* She waited, her mind on full alert. A barely discernible click caused Em to slide off the bed and stare at the door. *Was it Blackburn? Had he decided they should leave now?* As the door slowly opened, she clasped her hands together in trepidation.

Em froze in disbelief as the male form slid through the partially opened door. She had to be hallucinating. By the light from the chimney lamp and candle on the dresser, it looked like Josh. But it couldn't be. Josh was at the bottom of a cliff. He raised a finger to his lips as he set his shoes on the dresser. The gesture was unnecessary. Her tongue was frozen along with the rest of her body. Slowly, he walked toward her almost like he was afraid he might spook her. Em started trembling. Impossible, but it was Josh! He enfolded her with his arms, and she gripped his back, sobbing silently into his shoulder.

Ezra paused inside the doorway to allow Josh and Em a moment together. After a minute, he tapped Josh lightly on the arm. When Josh looked up, Ezra pointed to the door indicating that they should go. He mouthed the word "woods." Josh nodded. Pulling away from Em, he put his finger to his lips, grabbed his shoes, and pointed to the door. Em wiped her nose and eyes on the sleeve of her gown and nodded. Homer slid the door a little wider to let them pass and then closed it behind them.

Ezra set his shoes on the dresser, strode to the bed, and hurriedly removed the counterpane and bed linens. Homer set his shoes on the floor then rushed to the window. Unhooking the latch, he pushed the separated panes of glass outward. The cold night air rushed in, disturbing the candle on the dresser. Homer looked at Ezra who stood next to the stripped bed with a bedsheet in his hand staring at the bedpost. Both figured out at the same time that the bed was too far away from the window to support their illusion of Em climbing out the window.

Ezra crossed over to the table by the window. It probably wouldn't hold Em's weight as she climbed down, but hopefully Master Blackburn would be so furious he would not notice that small detail. Ezra tied a solid knot around the curved leg then tied the other sheet to the end of the first one. He yanked hard satisfied with the knot. Picking up the two bound sheets, he tossed them through the window. He looked over the edge to see how far they hung down. Only halfway, but it would have to do. As he turned back he heard the sound of a door latch. Both Negros froze for a long second, twin sets of fear etched on their faces.

Ezra snatched a brass candleholder off the table beside him and brought it down against the back of Homer's head.

He dropped like a stone and lay still. Ezra set the candleholder back on the table just as Blackburn opened the door clad in his billowy shirt and a pistol in his hand. Without taking time to think about his actions, Ezra grabbed a fistful of the sheet off the windowsill and swung out of the window just as Blackburn fired. He didn't have time to appreciate the irony of playing out this exact scene with Blackburn twice in a day and a half as the small table flew upside down and wedged itself against the window frame. The ball tore a small chunk out of a table leg as it whizzed through the window and out into the night sky.

Ezra quickly loosened his grip on the sheet and allowed gravity to pull him downward. The brick wall tore at his shirt as he looked up at the window. Blackburn was framed in the dim light of the window for a brief second and then was gone. Ezra knew he was coming to intercept him.

Ezra came to the end of the second sheet and let go. He landed at an angle on both of his shoeless feet and immediately a bolt of pain shot through his left ankle. He limped away from the brick wall and headed in the direction of the woods just as the ringing of a bell pealed incessantly. After three steps Ezra realized he would never reach the woods before Blackburn overtook him. The best he could do was to change direction and possibly throw Blackburn off on which way Josh and Miss Emily had gone.

Ezra turned right and limped as fast as his injured ankle could go.

"Halt!"

Ezra froze, afraid that the pistol was trained on his back with one ball still left, ready to end his life.

"Turn around in a slow manner."

Ezra pivoted around to face Blackburn. He could tell by the light of the moon that he did indeed have his double-barreled pistol trained on him. Out of the corner of his eye he saw movement as several male Negros converged on the scene. Despite the sharp pain in his ankle, he stared at Blackburn in defiance.

"You, Dembi, fetch some rope," Blackburn shouted.

Blackburn strode up to Ezra and pistol whipped him across the face, breaking Ezra's nose. Ezra gritted his teeth as the blood dripped onto ground. The slaves around him shifted uneasily as they awaited their master's bidding. Dembi returned with a piece of rope.

"Bind his hands."

Ezra felt the rope bite into his wrists as they were bound behind him. As he was led off, Ezra prayed that Josh and Miss Emily had reached the safety of the woods.

Josh paused at the servant's entry only long enough to put on his shoes. He and Em had almost reached the edge of the woods when they heard a gunshot. Josh stopped and pivoted toward the sound. His face, pale in the moonlight, showed his fear and indecision. Ezra had not deserted him on the ledge, but there was Em to consider.

Em sensed his indecision. "You go back. I'll find a good hiding place in the woods and wait on you.

"Em…"

"No. I don't know how you survived that fall, but I know you are here because of Ezra. Now go."

Josh had taken a step toward the house when the angry ringing of a bell pierced the night, followed by the pounding of feet and murmured voices. Josh changed direction and rushed Em into the darkness of the woods.

Once in the relative safety of the trees, both teens strained to see what was happening. The sound of a voice, shouting one word, reached them: "Halt."

Em gripped Josh's arm as he whispered, "He's still alive."

They could see dark shapes approaching the back of the mansion, but nothing else.

Josh stood there, the impulse to find out what happen warring with his need to get Em to safety.

"We have to help him."

Josh decision was made for him when several of the dark shapes headed in their direction.

"We will help him, but now we hide. Blackburn's sent out his slaves to look for us."

Trying to be as quiet as possible, Josh led Em back in the direction that he and Ezra had traveled earlier. He knew the road would be off to his right, but little else. He also knew if they attempted to walk too far through the woods in the dark they would get hopelessly lost. They needed a hiding place, somewhere Blackburn's slaves wouldn't find them. It had been a few years since he had been a boy scout, but Josh still remembered much of his outdoor survival training. One whole weekend just shy of his fourteenth birthday had been spent with his scout troop in the Croatian National Forest of North Carolina learning how to survive if you were lost in the woods.

Josh knew he had two choices as he crept beneath the budding leaves. Go up or go down. There would be no way to fight if they were discovered hiding in a tree so Josh searched the ground around them. A gap in the branches above them allowed a sliver of moonlight to illuminate a small area to their right. Two pine trees had been uprooted and landed on top of each other against the trunk of a hickory tree. Josh went to investigate, dragging Em with him. There was a gap between the pines and the hickory just spacious enough to accommodate the two of them if they snuggled close. Josh crouched to enter.

Em pulled back against Josh's arm. "No way. I'm not going in there with spiders and snakes and who knows what else in there."

Josh searched the ground until he found a foot-long stick. He ducked under some pine needles as he swished the branch back and forth trying to dispel any inhabitants. He didn't hear anything moving, so he fell to his knees and crawled into the small space. Man, it was a lot more cramped than it looked. His tall frame was bent double.

"Em, it's okay. Come on."

Em bent down peering in at Josh. "It doesn't look like there is enough room for me."

The sound of large animals crashing through the woods reached them. Em quickly fell to her knees and started to crawl in.

"No! That's not going to work," Josh whispered. "Turn around and back in."

Em flipped onto her rear end and scooted back into the enclosure butting up against Josh. She pulled her long legs in, hugging them to her chest.

They held their breath as footsteps grew close. One pair of footsteps walked right up to their hiding place. The pines pressed in against their knees as if hands were pressing on the trees.

"Dembi, I's sees sumpin."

The pressure evaporated and the footsteps faded into the woods. Josh and Em let out the breath they had held, at the same time. Em tried to shift her legs to the right away from a small twig digging into her shin.

"What should we do?"

"I really don't know, Em." Josh sighed. "We can't go back tonight with Blackburn on full alert and who knows how many of Blackburn's slaves guarding Ezra."

Josh reached up and pushed a twig full of pine needles out of his ear. "You try to sleep while I try to come up with a plan."

As Em laid her head on Josh's chest, she was more confused than ever. *What was God's purpose for them? Did he have one? Why were they still here?*

Ezra shut his eyes against the pain as Hattie squatted beside him with a wet rag to wipe the blood from his face. The bleeding had stopped, but he could feel the swelling of his nose. He sat propped against the rough wood of the kitchen wall, his hands tied behind his back and his legs encased in stockings splayed out in front of him. Pain exploded afresh as Hattie cleaned around his nostrils. He closed his eyes tighter. Emotions warred within him. He had never been physically abused until today. But he did not regret helping Miss Emily and Josh. Despite his pain he felt a fierce gratitude for Josh's friendship.

"I knows this hurts, but you's lucky this not too bad a break. You just be havin' a bump atop your nose." Hattie leaned back on her heels. "Now you tell me your name and whys you tied up like a …"

The kitchen door slammed open, and Blackburn entered with a large Negro in tow. Hattie jumped away from Ezra, knocking over a bucket as she backed toward the fireplace.

"Where is the lass?"

"I know not," Ezra muttered.

Blackburn scanned the room then walked over to the worktable where a sharp blade lay for cutting meat.

"Rise to your feet and sit down at the table."

With the male slave's help, Ezra pushed to his feet and sat down in a plain wooden chair. Blackburn indicated that the slave was to unbind Ezra's hands.

"Place both hands upon the table." Ezra did as instructed, trying to ignore the pain in his shoulders.

"I am going to ask you a number of questions. If I do not approve of the answer, I will cut off a finger."

Ezra swallowed, and his hands began to tremble.

"How did you gain entrance into my mother's bedroom?"

Ezra thought furiously then answered, "I knocked Homer insensible and searched his pockets. I discovered the key in one of the pockets."

"Were you alone, or was the lad with you?"

Head bent, Ezra closed his eyes as if in grief. "Nay, he fell into the river. I have not seen him."

Blackburn smiled at this bit of good news. He placed the knife atop Ezra's smallest finger of his right hand. "Please continue your tale."

"I opened the door and dragged Homer into the room and shut the door."

Blackburn drew the blade across the knuckle, and a bright spot of blood appeared. "And the lass?"

Ezra debated on his answer. The truth or a lie. He decided to stick closer to the truth. "I told her to run to the road while I tied the bed linens to the table to make it appear that the lass had climbed out the window and escaped on her own."

"Then the lass has not ventured far."

Ezra nodded miserably.

"Splendid! I have four slaves searching the woods and road now. They will bring her to me. And if they do not, I know where she will travel. She will go back to the bluff to look for her beloved. I will recapture her there and force her to give me the location of the jewels"

"She has no knowledge of the location of the jewels."

In one swift motion, Blackburn sliced off Ezra's finger above the knuckle. Ezra cried out in agony as he cradled the injured right hand in his left hand, blood pouring from the stump.

"I warned you of what would occur should I not like your answer."

"'Tis the truth." Ezra pressed his injured hand against his breastbone. The blood from his amputated finger was mixing with the dried blood from his nose that was caked to his dirty blouse. "When I jumped from the cliff, I grabbed a near branch and descended to the ledge. I discovered the pouch of jewels in a cleft in the cliff face behind a rock."

"'Tis a lie!" Blackburn shouted. "The lass described the pouch and jewels."

Blackburn reached for Ezra's hand. Ezra clutched his hand tighter and leaned back in his chair. "'Tis a trick! Only I know where the gems are hidden."

Blackburn paused. As much as he enjoyed torturing the traitorous Negro, with dawn fast approaching, he would need this black spawn of the devil conscious if the girl was not apprehended. He had no way of knowing whether it was the lass or slave that lied.

Blackburn turned to the Negro behind Ezra's chair. "Guard him until my return. If he escapes, your wench will be beaten."

As soon as the door closed, Hattie rushed to Ezra's side.

"Shows me that finger."

Ezra unclenched his left hand from his right. Blood was still pouring from the finger. Hattie placed the wet rag on top of the amputated stump and told Ezra to hold it there tight. She placed the knife that Blackburn had used to cut off part of Ezra's finger amongst the hot coals in the fireplace. She reached for some dried herbs hanging above her head. Pulverizing them with a mallet she mixed them into some grease. Carefully she lifted the hot knife from the coals.

"Takes off that rag. This is gonna hurt."

Ezra clamped his mouth tight against the scream that threatened as Hattie brought the searing blade across his bleeding finger to cauterize it.

"Now I's gonna put this poultice on it and wrap it up good and tight."

Ezra leaned his head back in the chair, tears rolling down his cheeks as Hattie covered the amputation with the salve.

The pain in Homer's side brought him back to consciousness. He was being kicked. He tried to turn away from the boot mercilessly attacking him.

"Stand, you worthless piece of manure!"

Recognizing his master's voice, Homer struggled to gain his feet. Once there he swayed against the pain in his head and side.

"Hie yourself to the kitchen and help Sam guard Ezra. If he escapes, I will add ten more lashes to your punishment of this eve."

Blackburn pivoted and left the room. Homer heard his bedroom door slam. As he stumbled toward the door, he tried to recall what had happened to him, but his head hurt too much. He placed a hand to his throbbing side and moved his fingers over the area. Nothing moved as if broken. Homer sighed with relief. He moved his fingers from his side to his head and immediately felt a bump that was very tender to his touch. He crossed the threshold and limped to the servants' entrance, his side hurting every time he placed his bare feet on the floor.

Homer made his way slowly up the outside steps and crossed the yard to the kitchen. He opened the door and glanced in. Ezra sat at the worktable, his head resting on his folded arms and a wooden cup of cider at his elbow. Sam sat across the table, eyes fixed on Ezra. Homer limped in, and Hattie rushed to his side.

"Homer! What's wrong with you?" She eased him into the old cane rocker in the corner of the kitchen.

As soon as Hattie said Homer, Ezra's head rose from his folded arms. "I am mighty sorry for the trouble I have put upon you, Homer."

"I'm not remembering what happen' to me." Homer flapped his arm at Hattie who was examining his head. "Stop making all this fuss."

She moved off to pour him a cup of cider.

Ezra lifted his own cup and took a sip. With an eye on Sam, he said, "I had to knock you out to allow Miss Emily to escape."

Confusion crossed Homer face, but he made no reply to Ezra. Instead he turned to Sam. "Masta sent me to helps you watch Ezra so he don't escape."

Sam muttered, "Masta said if this boy escapes, he gonna beat Effie. He ain't going nowhere."

Ezra closed his eyes and, mindful of his nose, laid his head back on his folded arms, his heart beating the same tattoo as his throbbing finger.

CHAPTER 15

J osh's eyes moved rapidly back and forth under his lids while he slept. He was dreaming about his best bud, Tim. He had met Tim on the same day he had met Em for the first time ten months ago. Josh's family had recently moved from Raleigh to Colonial Heights, and a teen girl on his block had befriended him. Thrilled to learn that Josh played basketball, Megan had invited him to shoot some hoops with a bunch of her friends on a Sunday after church. Josh accepted, and now Em was his girlfriend and Tim his best friend.

In his dream, he and Tim were playing one on one at the community court. And Tim was running circles around him, literally. Tim was rope thin, all hands and feet. The tight braids that lay in cornrows on top of his head glistened with sweat as he again avoided Josh's outstretched hand and drove to the net with a quick layup. Josh bent double, hands on his thighs breathing nosily through his mouth.

"Come on, dude, give me a break," Josh gasped.

"Josh, my man, just pretend this is a football field. I won't have a chance."

"Great idea. Next time you go for the dunk, I'll just tackle you and end this humiliation."

"Dude, I ain't coming to your pity party, you're only playing sappy songs."

Josh rose up laughing. "Come on, let's go to my house for dinner. Mom's ordering pizza."

Looping an arm across Tim's shoulders, they left the city park. As they arrived at the brick rancher that Josh lived in, Tim hung back, dribbling the basketball on the sidewalk while Josh crossed to the mailbox to retrieve the mail. Josh turned and strode up the walkway to the front door, but paused when he didn't hear Tim's footfalls behind him.

"Josh, I can't go with you."

Josh turned around. Tim stood at the end of the driveway. A tall young man in long navy sweat shorts and a white T-shirt, the basketball held rigidly in his arms.

"Josh, you gotta help my great-great-granddaddy, Ezra. If you don't, I won't be born."

Josh stared at Tim with a look of confusion on his face. "Tim, what are you talking about?"

Tim's form started to waver and grow dim. "Now, Josh, you've got to help him, right now!"

Josh woke with a start, his head bumping a branch and sending a shower of dead pine needles cascading down his face. Disoriented, it took him a minute to remember that he and Em had taken refuge behind the fallen pines to avoid being captured by Blackburn's slaves. The dream had faded rapidly, and all he could remember was that it had something to do with Tim and Ezra. He felt a sense of urgency he couldn't ignore.

Josh gently shook Em. "Em, wake up, we have to go."

Em's head snapped up, instantly alert. The last few days had sharpened her animal instincts. "Did you hear something?"

"No, it's Ezra, we have to go find him now."

Em could hear the fear in Josh's voice. "What's wrong?"

"I don't know…it's just that I had this weird dream, and I can't really remember, but it had something to do with Ezra. That he needs our help now."

"Was it like that vision I had about Martha?"

"I don't know, but all the sudden I am freaking out about Ezra."

"Okay, let's go."

Em rolled on her side and pushed her way out of the shelter with Josh close behind. Both struggled to their feet as circulation rushed back into their legs, causing a tingling sensation. They took baby steps in the direction they had come as the blood coursed back, feeding starved veins. After a couple of minutes, they could walk normally, picking their way gingerly through the darkness of the woods.

"What time is it?" Em whispered.

Josh pushed a button on his watch. "Three a.m."

"Are we going in the right direction?" Em whispered again.

"You don't have to whisper. The slaves have gone by now. And yes, I'm going in the right direction."

"Are you sure?"

Josh smiled into the dark. "Yes, I told you I was a boy scout, remember? But if you insist, I will stop and ask directions at the first raccoon we come across."

Em giggled, grateful to Josh for trying to lighten the mood for her sake.

"Oh, by the way, I found what Blackburn was so desperate to locate," Josh said.

"You found the jewels?"

"Wait a minute." Josh stopped and turned around. "How do you know about the jewels? Did Blackburn tell you?"

Em pushed on Josh's chest to get him moving. "No. You won't believe this, but I found another diary."

"You are kidding me."

Em brushed away a branch that pulled at her dress. "No, it was hidden in Blackburn's mom's vanity. There was a false bottom in the drawer. It's a fascinating story about how Blackburn's father came to posses the jewels. He stole them."

"What a surprise. The apple didn't fall too far from that tree."

"Well, I don't really blame him. There were extenuating circumstances."

"You can tell me all about it later." Josh slowed his gait as they approached the edge of the woods that bordered Blackburn's property.

"Where are the jewels?"

Josh turned his eyes, boring into Em's. "I'm not going to tell you, yet. The less you know, the safer you will be."

"But, Josh…"

"No buts. Now you stay here while I go and find out what Blackburn has done with Ezra."

"No way! I will not allow you to leave me again. Don't even try to argue."

Em's face shone with both fear and determination in the moonlight. There was no way she was going to stay behind. Josh accepted her decision.

"Okay, but you have to be as quiet as a mouse. And stay glued to my side."

Josh took a step out onto the lawn, trying to look in every direction at once. Not seeing any movement, he strode quickly toward the back of the mansion. Halfway, a movement caught his eye. The back door to the plantation house was opening. Josh grabbed Em's arm and pulled her to the ground.

"Ow!"

Josh covered Em's mouth with his hand and pressed her into the damp earth. Lucky for them, the door slammed shut as Em uttered her exclamation. Josh could tell it was Blackburn striding off in the direction of a small building a few yards' distance from the servants' entrance. He jumped up, pulling Em up with him.

Josh put his mouth close to Em's ear. "Sorry, Em, I didn't mean to hurt you, but we have to hurry."

Em had seen Blackburn and nodded. They hurried to the dwelling Blackburn had just entered. Smoke was rising from the chimney, and Josh guessed it to be the kitchen. Beside the door, there was a small window. A reddish glow wavered behind a piece of muslin cloth. Barely moving, Josh approached the lit window, Em in tow. Through a crack between the muslin and wooden frame, Josh could see Blackburn standing over Ezra with a gun in one hand and a coiled up length of rope in the other.

"I would relish putting this ball through your head, but as the lass was not apprehended, I must forgo that pleasure for another time."

Blackburn disappeared from Josh's view.

"Sam, tell Silas to hook up a horse to the cart and saddle my stallion."

Josh and Em quickly ducked around the side of the building as the door next to the window opened. Josh watched the slave rush off in the direction of the stables. He sidled back to the window. Blackburn had backed up to the wall opposite the window, his double-barreled pistol trained on Ezra. Josh knew if he burst through the door, he would be shot. He no longer doubted Blackburn's accuracy with his gun. He would have to wait until Blackburn exited the cook house and take him by surprise. He and Em moved back around the corner of the building out of sight.

Em mouthed, "What are you going to do?"

Josh whispered in her ear, "Take out Blackburn when he comes out. His back will be to us."

Em clenched Josh's arm in an iron grip. He placed a tender kiss of reassurance on her cheek.

Within ten minutes, Sam returned with the horse and cart. A young slave led the stallion.

Blackburn, hearing the sound of the cart's wheels, waved the pistol at Ezra. "Rise and face the door. Homer, bind his hands behind him."

Homer did as he was ordered.

"Now take him to the cart. One twitch and I shall have the pleasure of ending your life."

Josh braced himself against the corner of the log dwelling as the door opened. Ezra emerged limping to the cart, Homer's hand on his elbow. Blackburn emerged with his back to Josh. Before Josh could make his move a cat came out of the shadows of the mansion meowing with hunger. Blackburn turned as Josh ducked back behind the corner. When Josh peered back around the corner, Blackburn was too far away to tackle. Josh slumped against the rough wood in frustration.

"Ezra's in the cart," Em whispered.

Josh looked back around the corner.

"Sam, drive the cart," Blackburn ordered as he tossed the coil of rope on the bench seat of the cart. He crossed to his stallion and mounted, pocketing his pistol.

Sam climbed aboard the small seat of the two-wheeled cart as Homer returned to the cook house. He slapped the reins across the withers of the gelding as Blackburn kicked the flanks of his stallion. Josh was on the move before they were halfway down the drive, Em close behind. The young slave was making his slow way back to the stables. He had no idea that Josh was creeping up behind him.

As he took a step into the stable yard, Josh grabbed him from behind, covering his mouth with his hand. The boy, so slight a strong wind would blow him away, struggled as Josh picked him off his feet with one arm and carried him into the dimly lit interior of the stables. He looked around and nodded to Em and then to a strip of cloth lying on a stool. Em picked it up and wrapped it around her two hands. She walked up beside Josh and behind the stable boy. Lifting her arms she placed them over his head until the strip was even with the boy's mouth.

Josh looked sideways into Em's eyes, and she nodded. Josh removed his hand, and Em inserted the cloth in the boy's mouth before he released the scream in his throat. Quickly she tied the ends behind his head. Josh turned the terrified boy to face him. He was making guttural sounds in his throat.

Josh put a finger to his lips and said, "Shush!"

Immediately the boy became quiet.

"Em and I mean you no harm. We must borrow a horse. The slave in the cart is our friend, and Blackburn intends to kill him. Do you understand?"

The boy bobbed his head rapidly.

"I see two horses in the stalls. I need the one that is sturdy and reliable. And if you trick me, I will be very unhappy."

The slave shook his head no.

"If you make any noise saddling the horse, I will have to knock you out, understand?"

The boy's eyes, wide with terror, nodded again. Em could tell he had no intention of doing anything except what he was told. Josh let him go and watched warily as he silently coaxed a mare from one of the stalls. He laid a blanket across her back and then laid the saddle atop the blanket, cinching it tight. He glanced at Josh's height and lengthened the stirrups. He reached for a bridle hanging on a peg and pushed the mouthpiece against the mare's teeth until she accepted the inevitable and took it into her mouth. She shook her head once as the rest of the bridle went over her head and ears.

Em held the horse while Josh trussed the boy up like a Thanksgiving turkey with rope he had discovered hanging by a water bucket. He took the reins from Em and led the horse through the stable yard and onto the dirt track that lead to the road. Halfway to the road he stopped and mounted. He gripped the reins firmly in his right hand and then reached down with his left hand to help Em mount behind him. Josh slapped the reins lightly, and the mare set out at a trot, Em's arms wrapped around his waist.

"Now aren't you glad you went on those trail rides with me through the Shenandoah last fall," Josh said.

"I never said I didn't like the rides. I just said I was sore after we got off the horses," Em said to Josh's back. "And I'm enjoying this ride much better than the ride with Blackburn."

Josh turned left at the road, glad that the moon was bright enough to keep him from wandering from the road into the woods.

"Tell me what happened to you after I fell."

Em's head snapped up. "The fall! What happened! I thought you were dead. How did you survive?"

Josh looked toward heaven and smiled. "God saved me."

"I knew it! How did he do it?"

"Remember when we were arguing in the woods by Battersea and I was trying to get a signal on my cell but couldn't?"

Em nodded. "Yes."

"Well, instead of putting my cell phone in my breeches pocket where it was before, I slipped it into the little vest pocket. And when Blackburn shot me, the ball hit my cell phone. And instead of falling into the river, I landed on a ledge and was knocked out for a couple of hours. When I woke up, Ezra was beside me."

"God is good."

"All the time."

"Why do you think God has kept us here, Josh?"

"I…" Josh had a strong feeling that the answer was in the dream he had had earlier. He tried to remember, but all that came to mind was Tim's face and Ezra's. "I don't know. All I can think about is Ezra. He risked his life by jumping into the river to help me save you."

"He did what!"

"Yeah, a real *Indiana Jones* routine. You should have seen it."

Em tried to shift on the back of the saddle to a more comfortable position. "Josh, could we canter for a little bit, this trot is jarring my back."

Josh's voice was grim as he answered, "Sorry, Em, but we can't risk the mare stumbling in a deep rut. We should actually walk her to be safe, but we can't let Blackburn get too far ahead and kill Ezra before we get there."

Em sighed as she rested her cheek against Josh's back. It was all about trusting God, and she would do that—yes, she would.

——————

Blackburn looked up at the night sky as he turned his stallion's head toward the rutted drive on Banister's property. He had traveled behind the cart the full distance to be assured that Ezra did not attempt to jump and make haste for the woods. By the position of the moon, he still had time before daybreak and the arrival of the laborers. His eyes cased the trees on the property as he contemplated which one would best serve his purpose. The Negro would not be delivered from his fate this time. To the left of the villa stood a sturdy oak tree with a stout lower branch within reach if one stood upon the cart. Blackburn halted his horse at the hitching post and climbed down. He looped the reins three times around the rail.

"Sam, drive the cart to yon oak tree and halt beneath the lowest branch."

Sam clucked to the horse and pulled lightly on the left rein steering the cart beneath the branch as instructed.

Blackburn removed the pistol from his frock pocket. "Ezra, climb down and stand beside the tree."

Ezra did as instructed, limping to the tree and leaning on it for support.

"Sam, climb upon the cart and toss the rope over the branch." Blackburn watched as Sam obeyed. "Tie a firm hangman's noose."

Neither Blackburn nor Sam noticed Ezra start to tremble as he realized what lay before him. This was no threat to learn the whereabouts of the gems. How much torture he would suffer before death would depend on how much pain he could endure. He looked furtively around the acreage. Although he was very afraid for himself, he was more afeared that Josh and Em were concealed somewhere close and would be apprehended.

"Sam, position Ezra on his feet in the cart and slip the noose over his head."

All hope for escape left him. If he had not injured his ankle, Ezra would have run; instead he lowered his head in defeat. He could not climb into the cart with his hands bound behind him, so Sam lifted him until his knees rested on the wooden bed of the cart. Sam hoisted himself into the cart and jerked Ezra to his feet. He slipped the noose over his head, pulling it tight.

"Not too tight, Sam. I do not want the Negro to expire before I learn the location of my cache."

Sam loosened the knot and jumped down to the yard.

"Sam, take hold of the other end of the rope and stand behind the cart."

Ezra's eyes followed Blackburn as he walked to the side of the cart, returning the pistol to his pocket. His ankle, nose, and finger were all a vibrato of agony. He was very afraid, with the next wave of pain, he would pass out.

Blackburn's eyes had a maniacal gleam as he placed his hands on the wooden edge. "Raise the Negro a few inches and hold."

Ezra's eyes showed white in the incandescent glow as he was lifted from his feet and started to struggle.

CHAPTER 16

Josh pulled back on the reins as they approached the drive to the villa. He turned the horse into the line of trees bordering the property, ducking his head as a large branch loomed up in the dark. He climbed down from the horse then reached up to help Em down. He looped the reins over a branch and grasped Em's hand. Both crept to the edge of the drive and peered down the rutted path to the villa, standing dark and stark in the moon's luminous glow.

"Josh, there are large shadows beneath that tree on the left of the villa. I see someone moving."

"Yeah, I see them, but I can't make out what they're doing. Come on, we need to get closer." Trying not to alert Blackburn of their presence, Josh and Em moved at a snail's pace through the wooded area on the left side of the drive.

Josh's hand slipped into the pocket of his breeches. His fingers clasped the pouch with the jewels. He would give the jewels to Blackburn to save Ezra's life, but had no idea how to accomplish it. If he just handed them over, Blackburn would shoot the two of them without blinking. He had to make Blackburn let Ezra go first.

Josh's head started to pound rapidly along with his heart. He would never let it show to Em, but he was scared out of his mind for Ezra. The bond he had formed with Ezra in the last two days was every bit as strong as the one he had with his friend, Tim. He was not going let him die!

Em startled him by giving his wrist a soft yank. "We're close, I hear a voice."

Josh brought his mind back to the immediate present and released the gems. Moving aside low sprigs, he strained to hear who was talking.

Em leaned in close to Josh's ear. "Sounds like Blackburn. I heard Ezra's name and something about his feet."

They continued to creep closer. Josh could hear Blackburn instructing Sam to stand behind the cart with a rope. As they approached the last bit of tree cover, they heard Blackburn tell Sam to raise the Negro.

His view now unobstructed by branches and trees, Josh's heart jumped into his throat. Ezra was hanging by his neck struggling to breathe, his feet dangling a few inches above the bed of the cart. But before he could react, Blackburn told Sam to lower Ezra to the cart. Josh watched Ezra collapse behind the wooden sides of the cart. He judged the distance to the tree. It was too far away to make a surprise attack. Blackburn would have plenty of time to pull his pistol and shoot. Josh grabbed the bark of the nearest tree with both hands. His rage was so great, his fingers started to bleed. Beside him he could hear Em crying softly.

In a furious whisper, Josh said, "I am going to get him, Em. If it is the last thing I do, I'm going to make that sick psychopath pay."

Looking at Josh's face, Em knew he meant every word, and her fear increased for both Ezra and Josh. She had to do something. A diversion of some sort. *Think, Em, think.*

"I do hope being strung up by the neck was a significant enough event to get your attention."

Blackburn placed both arms behind his frock coat and grasped his hands together as he stared down at the prone figure of Ezra in the bed of the cart. "Where are the gems concealed?"

Ezra's fear had disappeared and been replaced by a searing rage that encompassed his whole body. He would most assuredly die, but before that occurred, he would relish sending Blackburn on as many wild-goose chases for the gems as possible.

"'Tis hidden beneath the large stone betwixt the drive and the road," he gasped out.

Blackburn stared up the rutted track to the road, but could see no stone in the dim light cast by the moon. "Sam, hasten to the road and search out the stone. Seek beneath it for a small pouch and bring it to me."

As Sam ran to the road, Josh leaned back against the oak tree in relief. "Good going, Ezra," he whispered.

The next few minutes were agony for Josh and Em as each concentrated on a way to free Ezra. Josh turned to Em, motioning her back into deeper cover.

"I'm going to draw Blackburn's fire while Sam is by the road."

"No! Absolutely not! You don't have nine lives. He could kill you this time," her whisper came out in a hiss.

Josh gripped Em by the shoulders. "It's dark and I'll be moving. He won't hit me."

Tears were rolling down Em's cheeks. "No, there has to be a better plan." She wrapped her arms around Josh's neck and held on tight.

"There isn't, Em, and you know it." Josh pulled away as footsteps pounded by their hiding place.

"What the...?" Josh clenched his fist in frustration. "How did he get back so fast?"

Josh and Em crept back to their position at the tree line. Sam was trying to talk between great heaving breaths. "Masta', I's found...the stone...but there aint...no pouch under that... stone."

Ezra spoke from the wagon, "Those gems are there. He did not search adequately."

"You have played me for the fool for the last time!" Blackburn shouted over the side of the cart at Ezra. "I am going to deprive you of an ear. And for each lie henceforth, I will remove a body part."

Blackburn reached into his boot and removed his knife as Josh and Em looked on in horror. "Sam, restrain his movements."

Without conscious thought, Em shouted "No!" and ran into full view of Blackburn. Josh tried to grab her arm but missed. Realizing her mistake of running toward Blackburn, she turned right and ran toward the road.

"Sam, pursue the lass! Do not let her elude you!" Blackburn yelled.

Josh started to run after Em and Sam, but changed his mind. He was big, but Sam was bigger. If he fought Sam and was knocked out, all was lost. He knew Sam wouldn't hurt Em because Blackburn wanted her. He said a quick prayer for God to give Em swift feet. *Oh, and a little help for me too.* He had decided to show Blackburn the jewels, now. Once he did, all of Blackburn's attention would be focused on Josh, and maybe Ezra could get away. But he needed some kind of shield, something to deflect a bullet like the cell phone only bigger.

Josh crouched and scanned the area around him, but there were only branches, which did him no good. He could actually feel his window of opportunity shrinking by the minute. His anxiety increased. Blackburn now had his pistol out again and trained on Ezra. Desperately, his eyes scanned the area beyond the edge of the woods. And then he glimpsed it, a flat rock reflecting moonlight. His prayer answered! He would have to be quick. Blackburn could get a shot off before he reached the rock.

Josh took a deep breath and charged from the cover of the trees, his muscular legs pumping like two pistons. He heard the crack of the pistol and dove for the rock like he was sliding into home plate at his high school field. The ball whistled over his head as he twisted and brought the rock up to his chest breathing hard. Blackburn now had one hand on the pistol trained on Josh and one on the cart horse's halter, trying to restrain him from bolting. The horse was shaking his head and snorting nervously. Josh scrambled to his feet, the stone held before his midsection ready to move up or down to deflect the ball. Even from a distance he could tell that Blackburn was shocked.

"How the devil did you survive the impact of the ball and the fall from yon bluff!"

"I tell you what, tomorrow when this is all over, we'll have tea and I'll tell you all about it. But meanwhile I have something of interest to you."

Holding the rock with one hand, he reached into his breeches pocket and pulled out the pouch. "I have your jewels."

Josh knew Blackburn's shock had morphed into rage. He could see the hand holding the gun trembling as he dropped the other from the horse. He even knew what he was thinking. He had one bullet left; what if he missed?

As Josh returned the jewels to his pocket, he had a sudden image of his seventy-year-old grandfather and himself hunched over a chessboard in deep concentration over their next move. *What we have here*, Josh thought, *is a stalemate*.

———⊕———

Em ran as fast as she could for the road hoping that with Sam chasing her, Josh could come up with a plan to neutralize Blackburn without getting shot. She repeated *Please, Lord, please,*

Lord over and over in her mind as she ran. And then the chase was over. A few yards from the road, her right foot slipped on the wet dew, and her feet went out from under her. Em's jarring impact with the earth knocked the wind out of her and sent a wave of pain through her back. She would have groaned in pain if she could have breathed. A large shadow loomed over her, blocking out her view of the stars overhead. Sam's huge hands reached down and clamped onto her arms, jerking her to her feet. Em didn't even have enough breath to protest his rough treatment.

In one swift move, Sam lifted her and slung her over his shoulder. The one breath she had finally been able to take whooshed out as soon as her abdomen slammed into his shoulder. Despite the pain in her back, Em began to struggle, trying to slow Sam down as much as possible. Her feeble effort had no effect as Sam took off in an easy lope back toward the villa. Em repeated the litany she had been reciting on her run for the road: *Please, Lord, please, Lord.*

Ezra lay in the cart taking shallow breaths and struggling to rise to a seated position so he could observe what could only be a foolhardy rescue attempt by Josh and Miss Emily. He knew Sam was chasing Miss Emily and that the shot from the pistol was aimed at Josh. But he had heard no cry. Maybe Josh was unhurt. He scooted his body back against the sideboards using his bound hands as leverage to shift on to his backside as Master Blackburn and Josh exchanged words. Sweat popped out on his forehead, and his vision started to dim with the effort. He stopped and took as deep a breath as possible through his painful throat. He increased the pressure on his arms as he inched his backside to the right. He took another breath and with the last of his strength jerked upright. The cart creaked with his effort; the horse in his harness snorted.

Ezra glimpsed Blackburn glance in his direction then turned his attention back to Josh. He could see the concentration on Master Blackburn's face, waiting for Josh to make a mistake and give him a clear shot. Turning his head, he tried to locate Josh. The rope sawed into his neck, and he stopped. He must free himself to assist his friend!

"Blackburn, shoot your gun into the ground and I will give you the jewels," Josh said.

"It would be exceedingly foolish to comply with your request," Blackburn said with scorn.

Ezra struggled desperately to unbind his hands. The cords on his neck stood out against the rope as he strained to release his hands. Movement caught his eyes. Sam strode into view with Em slung over his shoulder. His mouth flattened into a grim line as he doubled his efforts.

Sam pulled Em off his shoulder, dropping her in a puddle at his feet. Blackburn picked up the knife he had dropped to grab the cart horse's halter and shoved it back into his boot. He strode to Em and yanked her to her feet. With a self-satisfied grin, he brought the pistol up to her temple. Blackburn glanced over at Ezra as he twisted to his knees and tried to push to his feet.

"Sam, it does appear as if Ezra wishes to gain his feet. Pull the rope taut to assist him."

Ezra felt himself being pulled up, the rope strangling him until he gained his feet, and then the rope slackened again.

"Now, lad, your choice." Blackburn's voice was rich with triumph. "Shall I hang the Negro or shoot the lass?"

CHAPTER 17

J osh's mind went blank with shock. Ezra stood with the noose around his neck and his face full of defiance. Em was plastered against Blackburn, the pistol to her head and her face a mixture of fear and anger. And then suddenly into the void a voice quoted scripture. *Trust in the Lord with all your heart and lean not on your own understanding.* He frowned and then he understood. *Things are not always what they seemed.*

"Shall I make the decision for you? The dawning of the day is imminent, and I grow weary of these games," Blackburn said.

He knew it was just an illusion, but Josh suddenly felt as if his body was being encased with armor. His decision already made, Josh's voice carried the conviction of his faith. "I will trust in the Lord."

In the seconds it took Blackburn to puzzle and then react to Josh's statement, Ezra noticed that Sam had removed one hand from the rope and that the other hand was slack, as he slapped an annoying bug away from his face. Ezra took one step and launched himself, feet first, at Sam. His attention on the infuriating insect buzzing in front of his eyes, Sam did not see Ezra jump from the cart, but he did glance down as he felt the rope tug through his fingers. Before he could react, Ezra's feet slammed into his stomach, and he fell with a thud, his head colliding with the hard ground. Stunned, he lay there without moving, Ezra on top of him gasping for breath.

Blackburn jerked around at the sound of Sam crashing to the ground, pulling the gun away from Em's head. In the instant that the gun pulled back from her temple, Em turned sharply and kneed Blackburn in his groin. Blackburn's knees buckled, but he did not release Em or the pistol. Em grabbed for the gun and missed as her knees slammed into the ground by Blackburn.

The minute Em kneed Blackburn, Josh took off, the flat stone held out in front of him. On his knees and in pain, Blackburn saw Josh running toward him, took aim at his head, and fired. The horse reared and took off, the cart clattering across the mole tunnel hills and tufts of new grass. As the ball's momentum carried it on a straight course to Josh's head, his hands holding the rock rose as if of their own accord. The bullet deflected harmlessly off the stone and to the right. Blackburn tried to reach into his boot for his knife, but Em yanked his hand away. Josh reached his adversary and with arm muscles bulging raised the rock and brought it down on top of the tricorn hat resting on Blackburn's head. Blackburn's eyes rolled up, and he fell forward, his hand releasing Em.

Josh dropped the rock and gripped Em's arm, helping her to her feet. He pulled her into his arms, holding her tight. Em grabbed Josh's shoulders, weak with relief.

"Are you okay?" Josh murmured into Em's disheveled auburn hair.

She pulled back and took a deep breath. "I'm okay." Suddenly, her eyes widened. "Ezra!"

Both turned and rushed the few feet to Ezra's side. He laid prone, his legs and feet resting on Sam's chest. He wheezed as he tried to draw breath. Em fell to her knees and using both hands slipped her fingers between the rope and Ezra's neck. She tried to pull it away so Ezra could breathe. Josh bent to one knee behind Ezra's head. He grabbed the rope forcing it through the knot. As the noose widened, Em worked it up and over Ezra's neck. Ezra took a deep breath and gasped.

Josh rose and gripped Ezra under the shoulders pulling him off Sam and into a seated position. He bent down to the rope binding Ezra's hands and tried to untie it, but it was too tight from Ezra trying to jerk free his hands. Josh rose to his full height and looked about for something to cut the rope.

Em guessed what Josh was looking for. "Josh, get the knife in Blackburn's boot!"

Josh ran back to Blackburn and reached a hand into the boot on Blackburn's right foot and pulled out the knife. He rushed back to Ezra and sawed the rope apart. Ezra brought his arms to the front of his body, moving them around to relieve the cramping. His breathing was laborious, but enough air was finally getting in and filling his lungs. Ezra raised his arm in a gesture of needing assistance. Josh helped him up and grasped him tight, slapping him on the back as Ezra grimaced in pain.

He pulled back and wiped his wet eyes. "Thank you, my man, for having my back. I owe you big-time."

Em rose and put arms around Ezra also. "Thank you, thank you, for saving our lives. You are a hero."

Ezra backed out of his friends' embrace, rubbed his abraded throat, and croaked out, "Nay... Miss Emily, I am not...a hero, but it was an honor...to be of assistance to you and Josh."

"We beg to differ...hey, what happened to your nose?" In the moonlight, Josh could tell it had doubled in size. "And why is your little finger wrapped up?"

"'Tis nothing...that will not heal...Josh. Do not concern yourself."

Ezra swallowed a lump that had nothing to do with the hangman's noose. "You both risked...your lives...to...release me, and I am exceedingly grateful."

The teens turned as a groan escaped from between Sam's lips. Josh's grip tightened on the knife in his hand. Sam shook his head, turned onto his side, and pushed to his knees. He rose and stumbled to his left. His eyes widened when he saw Blackburn facedown in the weedy patch of dirt.

He looked at the teens. "What you done to the masta'?"

Ezra eyes had been casing the acreage. When he turned them upon Sam, they had hardened like chips of coal. He took in as deep a breath as he could and pointed with his finger to the west. "Sam, retrieve the horse and...cart. Return them to your master's home and we will not harm you." Ezra forced more air through his tortured throat. "If you attempt to harm us, Effie will become a widow by dawn."

Sam stood undecided. The masta's wrath would be great when he returned, but the young white boy held the masta's blade, which was long and wickedly sharp. He knew. He had honed it himself. Sam heaved a long sigh and trudged across the property to the west, his head pounding and his stomach sick.

Ezra, Josh, and Em had not noticed the night sky turning to a pearl gray as morning approached. Sam arrived at the cart and hauled his body up and onto the bench seat, slapping the reins. As the horse started to trot back toward the road, they finally turn their attention to Blackburn.

"Is Master Blackburn dead, Josh?" Ezra asked.

"Don't know and seriously don't care."

"Josh!" Em admonished.

Josh's blue eyes blazed. "Well, I don't! He almost killed you and Ezra. He would have killed Martha, you saw it in your vision. And he raped who knows how many women. I think God would understand how I feel."

Em grasped Josh's hand. "And I do, too."

All three tensed when Blackburn coughed into the ground.

Josh looked at his new friend with resignation. "Well, Ezra, my man, I guess that answers your question. The spawn of Satan is alive. Hand me the rope and we can tie him up. We'll just have to explain it all to Colonel Banister when he arrives."

As Ezra took a couple of steps and reached down for the rope, Em's hand tightened on Josh's. "Josh! Do you feel it?"

"What?" Josh looked at Em in puzzlement.

"I'm feeling lightheaded. I think we're going back!" Em's voice rose with excitement.

"Wait! You're right, I'm feeling lightheaded too."

Ezra limped back with the noose in his hands and the rope trailing behind him.

Josh's elation turned to fear. "No, we can't go yet! We have to be here to explain to Colonel Banister about Blackburn, or Ezra will hang."

"What say you, Josh?" Ezra said.

"It's happening now. Em and I are going back to our time," Josh replied.

Em turned to Josh. "We could take Ezra back with us to our time. Then he'll be safe."

On the ground, Blackburn stirred and moaned.

"Ezra, take my hand. You'll be safe with us, and we will take care of you," Josh implored.

Ezra's smile was sad, but also full of hope. "Nay, Josh, you are bound for home, and I am bound for Boston and freedom's road. I shall not live long enough to witness the end of slavery, but if I live a good, long life, I shall glimpse the coming dawn of that fine day. I thank you with abundant joy for your friendship! I shall always remember and keep you and Miss Emily in my prayers each eve before I lay my head to rest."

The dizziness increased as Josh's voice rose in desperation. "Even if you tie up Blackburn, one of the laborers will set him loose when they arrive, and he will catch you."

"God will watch over me as he has watched over you," Ezra said, his faith absolute.

"But…"

Em tugged on Josh's arm to get his attention. "I know another way to keep Ezra safe."

Josh looked at Em in confusion, her form starting to waver as the vertigo hit in nauseous waves.

Em pointed at Blackburn. "We take him with us."

Josh's grin was pure delight. "Quick, Em, grab an arm."

Both rushed to Blackburn, dropped to their knees, and grabbed a forearm. Josh looked back up at Ezra a few feet away. "There is a horse hidden in the woods by the road. You take it. Blackburn won't have need of any of his possessions."

Salty tears flowed down Josh's face. He swallowed to still the bile threatening to rise from his stomach. Ezra was now but a wavering shadow. "You are my fine friend, Ezra and I love you."

Em cried freely. She smiled and gave Ezra a thumbs-up as her vision dimmed and then disappeared altogether. Em passed out against Blackburn's back still grasping his arm. She was vaguely aware that Josh had done the same.

The dawning of the new day sun cast a shimmering glow over his friends as Josh and Em disappeared back to their time, taking Blackburn with them. Ezra stared in amazement, his eyes glistening with emotion. He reached into his breeches pocket for his bit of muslin to wipe his wet eyes. His forehead creased in puzzlement. Ezra's hand pulled out the damaged cell phone. The grin was huge on his nut-brown face. It had survived his jump into the river. He now had a remembrance from his friend, Josh.

Ezra glanced down at his other hand holding the noose. His elongated fingers rubbed the roughness. He uncurled his hand and let it drop to the ground. When he looked back up, he noticed Master Blackburn's horse tied to the hitching post. He needed to buy time before anyone started questioning the whereabouts of Master Blackburn.

Ezra limped to the horse, untied him, and led him to the line of trees beside the property. He walked him a goodly amount of yards in, until he was well hidden, and tied the reins to a stout branch. He rubbed the velvety nose and whispered, "You're welcome."

Ezra limped through the trees wincing in pain. He came upon the mare cautiously, reaching up to rub her ears. He took the reins and walked her to the edge of the road, pausing as he heard the sound of horse hooves. A cart was coming from the direction of Petersburg with the first laborers. Ezra retreated back into the trees. After the cart had turned onto the property, Ezra took a deep breath in through the soreness of his throat and mounted the mare. He kicked her lightly in the withers and she moved on to the road.

Ezra paused on the road for a moment and then pulled on the right rein instead of the left. He had made a decision. He would make one detour to pick up Homer, provisions for the road, and glancing down at his hose-covered feet, shoes. With his master gone, Homer may be more amenable to Ezra's proposition than he had previously. As he kicked the mare into a fast trot, he realized he was now on his journey toward freedom. An indescribable joy filled him. With a shout, he kicked the mare again and galloped down freedom's road.

CHAPTER 18

APRIL 2009

Gunfire resonated around her as Em slowly gained consciousness. Her confused mind thought, *Gunshots?* And then, *Is Blackburn shooting at Josh?!* Her eyes snapped open, and she jerked upright, looking around her in terror. *Josh, where was Josh!* She flipped around to look behind her and saw Blackburn facedown on the floor beside her and Josh sprawled on his back beside him. *Josh!* Her fingers frantically searched his body for a wound. Finding no sign of blood, she checked for breathing and a heartbeat as her own heart pounded like a trip hammer in her chest. She could see his chest moving up and down and could feel his breath on the palm of her hand when she pressed it close to his nose. She gave a sigh of relief. Her fear subsided enough to be able to take in the sights and sounds around her.

Em could still hear the gunshots, and they were deafening. *Some kind of battle?* She pushed to her feet, ignoring the wave of dizziness, as she crossed to a large window, placing her fingers on the glass. Through the window she could see redcoats and patriots in a heated gunfight. Her brain finally caught up with what her fingers were feeling. *Panes of glass?* Em whirled around.

The display table, two metal chairs, brick showing through the plaster—she was back in the room of the east wing! Em whooped and twirled. *We're back—thank you, God—we're back!*

Em's eye caught sight of the damaged floor plank, and she stopped spinning. She walked slowly to the hole and knelt down. Her hand shook as she placed it in the hole. Em felt around, but there was nothing inside the cavity but packed dirt. She breathed a sigh of relief and looked up toward heaven with a thankful heart. Martha had grown up and probably married and had children of her own.

Em's head jerked in Josh's direction at the sound of a moan. She couldn't be sure if it had been Josh or Blackburn. *Blackburn?* The word slammed into her brain, and Em leaped to her feet. *It worked!* They had brought Blackburn back with them. And right on the heels of that thought came another as Em's eyes widened. *Oh no, what were they going to do with him? He was still as dangerous as a pit viper, pistol or no pistol. And what if he regained consciousness before Josh?* She stood frozen with indecision, and then Josh moaned again.

Em rushed over to Josh. "Josh, can you hear me? You have to open your eyes."

Josh's eyelids fluttered and then opened. He squinted up at Em. "I…Em?"

"Yes, it's me. It's okay, we're back."

Josh tried to push himself up. Em grabbed an arm and pulled. Once he was in a seated position, Josh placed both hands on either side of his head. "My head feels like it's double its normal size."

Em smiled. "Not a fan of time travel?"

"What?" The total confusion on Josh's face made Em laugh for the first time in what seemed like days.

"And what is all that gunfire?" Josh said in irritation.

"Oh, that's the reenactment of the Battle of Petersburg we were hoping to miss," Em said.

Em's face took on a mischievous expression. "What do you think we should do with Blackburn?"

"Blackburn?"

"Yeah, Blackburn, you're leaning up against him."

Josh dropped his hands and turned. He yanked his body away from the man on the floor, and Em watched as different expressions flitted across Josh's face. First, came confusion, then fear and anger as his memories of their trip back in time returned, and finally triumph as the realization hit that it had worked and they had brought Blackburn back with them. Josh rose unsteadily to his feet with Em's help and looked around the room.

"We really are back!" Em could hear the wonder in his voice.

"Josh, how do you feel?"

Josh took in a deep breath and let it out slowly. "Better, my head feels normal again and only a little headache."

Josh's steely gaze bore holes in Blackburn's back, and his face hardened. "I am going to pound him into the pavement."

He took one step, and Em grabbed his arm. "No! You can't."

"Why not!" His body shook with the rage he was feeling. "He tried to hang Ezra!"

"I know, but if someone saw you beating on him, they're going to arrest you. No one here knows what Blackburn did."

Josh relaxed his fists. "You're right."

Josh actually smiled and looked down at Blackburn. "So much for your precious jewels. They won't do a thing for you in this century."

Josh's eyebrows reached up for his hairline. "Oh, man! The jewels."

He quickly reached into his pocket, and his whole face lit up when he pulled out the pouch. "They came back with me!" Josh whooped his joy, which was drowned out by the fierce battle still being reenacted on the east lawn of Battersea.

Em stared in shock. "You had them the whole time?"

"Yep."

"And, you didn't tell me?" Em socked Josh in the arm.

"Ow! It was for your own good." Josh loosed the broken leather throng and upended the gems. Each, the size of a walnut, sparkled in the palm of Josh's hand.

"Oh, they are so beautiful! Can I hold them?" Em asked.

Josh dropped them onto Em's eager palm. "An emerald, ruby, and sapphire!"

She caressed each stone with the index finger of her left hand and then looked down at Blackburn. Reluctantly she gave them back to Josh. He returned them to the pouch and put them in his pocket.

"What are we going to do with them and Blackburn?" Nervously, she eyed Blackburn again. "Why isn't he coming to? Do you think he's dead?"

Josh bent down and grasped Blackburn's frock coat with both hands and flipped him onto his back. Then he bent down on one knee and pressed his head up against Blackburn's chest.

"His heart's beating. He's alive."

As if to prove Josh's point, Blackburn jerked involuntarily. Josh jumped to his feet and moved back a foot.

"He's probably taking longer to wake up because I slammed that stone on his head."

"What are we going to do about him?" Em said anxiously. "As soon as the battle's over, people will start wandering through the villa again. And whoever is manning the display table will be back."

Josh thought about that for a minute. "Okay, this is my idea. We go get someone in charge and tell them we found this man passed out on the floor. They take him to the hospital. He wakes up ranting and raving about his jewels and talking crazy and they put him in the loony bin." Josh started to grin and then stopped at the look of fear on Em's face.

Blackburn started to moan and kick his feet. Em grabbed Josh's arm.

"Oh, no, Josh! We have the jewels. It doesn't matter what century it is. Blackburn will say we took his jewels and we have no proof they're ours. How would two teenagers get their hands on stones like these? We'll be arrested!"

"We could say we found them, which is the truth. We just won't tell anyone which century we found them in, otherwise we will be patients in the same loony bin with Blackburn, and I do not want my big decision on any given day to be cherry Jell-O or chocolate pudding."

Despite her fear, Em laughed. That was what she loved about Josh. He could lighten up any serious circumstance. "Cute, you know you love…" Em paused. The gunfire had stopped and Em could hear voices coming their way through the outside door of the east wing.

"Josh, quick the jewels! Take them out of your pocket. I have an idea."

Josh pulled the pouch out of his pocket just as Blackburn started to stir to wakefulness. Both watched anxiously as his eyes started to open.

"Oh, there you are," Sally said as she climbed the few steps of the east wing porch and strode into the room followed by Ann. "I came to relieve you at noon, but you had disappeared.

You have no idea how right you are, Josh thought as they turned around.

Sally stared at the teens in shock. "My goodness, what happened to your costumes?"

Em's relief was palatable. She had prayed it would be Sally or Ann that came through the door and not a tourist. Since neither woman had mentioned the man on the floor, Em figured their bodies must be blocking their view of Blackburn. They could deal with him in a few minutes. First, the jewels.

"It's a long story, but guess what Josh just found in the hole over there! He was curious and bent down to look in the gap in the floor and…give them the pouch, Josh!"

Josh handed it to Ann. "It's three gems. Sorry, I know we shouldn't have, but we looked inside."

Em could hear Blackburn behind them moving around as Ann opened the pouch and glanced inside. "Take them over by the display table. The light's better."

As Ann gently extracted the jewels and laid them one by one on the table, Josh looked back at Blackburn, who was sitting on the floor with his legs crossed and holding his head.

"Oh, my goodness, they are magnificent!" Ann and Sally said together.

Both looked over to Josh.

Ann said, "You found them in that gap in the corner?"

"Yes, ma'am."

Ann's grin was huge. "This will really help with the restoration."

Another lady dressed in eighteenth-century garb walked in. "Sally, I'm back to help you with the brochures. Hey, what have you got there?" Her eyes widened, and her mouth formed a perfect O.

"Josh found them in the hole over there in the corner of the room," Sally said.

"Sir, are you okay? Did you fall?"

Everyone in the room turned to look as a man in his early twenties dressed similar to Josh came across the threshold from the room to the left. He walked over to Blackburn as he struggled to get his feet beneath him and stand up. The young man reached a hand down to help.

Blackburn brushed off the hand. "Do not touch me, commoner."

The man backed off with a frown on his face. Josh had taken Em's hand, tugging on it as he took backward steps to the outside door of the east wing. Both stepped over the threshold and onto the porch as Blackburn struggled to stand. Once upright, he yanked down on the bottom edge of his frock coat with both hands. He stared around the room in confusion. His left hand rose to push a stray raven lock out of his eye.

"How did I come to be in this room? I do not recall entering the villa."

Josh and Em watched as the man and three ladies looked at each other then shrugged their shoulders.

"We have no idea, sir," Sally said.

"Where is Banister?"

"Oh, this ought to be good," Josh whispered in Em's ear.

"Banister?" Sally queried.

"Mister Banister. The owner of this villa," Blackburn snapped.

"We didn't have anyone sign up to act as Colonel Banister this year," Ann said.

Blackburn glared. "Do not vex me, woman, with your talk of nonsense." His tone bristled as he suddenly noticed Ann's beige slacks and white shirt. "How dare you stand in my presence dressed as a common strumpet in her bedchamber?"

Everyone in the room and on the porch took a collective breath and held it.

"Hey, that was uncalled for. I don't care if you are trying to act as close to the time period as you can. You owe the lady an apology and then you need to leave," the man in the room said.

Blackburn turned on the man in outrage. "How dare you speak to me thus! I shall see you arrested and thrown in gaol."

The man addressed the room, "Do you know who is in charge here?"

Ann answered, "I am. I'll find a couple of the soldiers from Fort Lee that have been assisting today and have him escorted off the property." She turned to scoop the jewels back into the pouch.

As Ann turned, Blackburn was given a clear view of the table.

"Those are my gems!" Blackburn shouted. "Wench, give them to me, at once! You shall hang for stealing my property."

The woman in the period costume next to Sally said, "That man has a serious screw loose. We need to call 911." She pulled a cell phone out of the pocket of her dress and punched in the three numbers.

Blackburn strode over to Ann as she put the last gem in the pouch and snatched it out of her hand. The young man rushed over and seized his arm. Blackburn jerked it free and turned to the outside door. At the sight of Em and Josh, he froze. First, confusion distorted his face and then rage. He reached in his boot for his knife but discovered that it was missing. He looked up at Josh.

"Sorry, dude, left it in the eighteenth century. I borrowed it to free Ezra's hands."

"Josh, shush," Em said as she elbowed him in the ribs.

Blackburn raised his arm, holding up the pouch in triumph. "All your manipulations have come to naught. 'Tis my cache. I shall locate Fletcher or Banister, and you and your cohorts will soon be on your way to the gaol in Williamsburg. And wherever that Negro has fled I shall find him and observe him hang."

"That's what they call a pipe dream, dude. Get used to it. With all the drugs you're going to be on, you'll have lots of dreams. But if I had my way they'd all be nightmares," Josh said.

The woman next to Sally snapped her cell phone shut. "Police are on the way. They said about five minutes."

"Let me pass," Blackburn ordered Josh and Em.

"No can do, my man. You have an appointment with the men in the white coats."

Blackburn turned and walked toward the other door. The man in his twenties ran over and blocked it with his body.

"Step aside, commoner, or you will join the lad and lassie as their necks are stretched on the gallows."

"Like..." The man looked at Josh, a question in his eyes.

"Josh," Josh said.

"Right, my name is Jarrod."

"Like Josh said, there is a room up at Eastern State Hospital with your name on it."

Blackburn turned back toward Josh, his face as red as a beet. "I will see that you hang slowly for these repeated insults."

Sirens could be heard in the distance coming closer, which caused Josh to grin widely. "I'd love to continue with this stimulating conversation, but that noise you are hearing means this party is over."

Josh looked at Jarrod. "Jarrod, my man, do you think you could hold this fine gentleman while I retrieve the pouch of jewels, which is the property of the Battersea Foundation."

"That would be my pleasure."

Jarrod leapt forward and wrapped two strong arms around Blackburn, pinning his arms to his sides. As Blackburn struggled, Josh ran over and yanked the pouch from Blackburn's fist. He ran over and gave the pouch back to Ann. Through the window he saw a Petersburg police cruiser come to a stop at the front porch and two policemen open the driver and passenger doors.

"Unhand me, you clod, this instant! And return my property!" Blackburn shouted furiously.

"Not a chance."

"Cops are about ten seconds away. Need any help?" Josh asked with a grin.

"Pleasures all mine." Jarrod grunted.

Footsteps sounded in the next room, and four seconds later, the two cops passed through the portico. They veered around Jarrod and Blackburn until they faced both.

"You can let go of the gentleman now, sir. We'll take it from here," the taller of the two policemen said.

As Jarrod released Blackburn, the policeman continued to speak, "I am Officer Jackson, and this is Officer Dewitt. It is our understanding that you are disturbing the peace."

Em walked back into the room with Josh as Blackburn stared at the two cops in rage and confusion.

Officer Jackson looked around the room. "I need to know which person called in the complaint."

The woman next to Sally raised her hand, and Officer Dewitt walked over to get her statement.

Blackburn finally spoke, "What manner of dress do you wear?"

"This is my uniform," Jackson said in a calm manner.

"Uniform? Are you an officer of the court?"

"That is one of my duties."

"I have never seen a member of the court dressed thusly."

Em saw the uneasiness in Blackburn's eyes as he stared at the policeman. She could tell he was beginning to understand that things were not as they should be in his everyday world. Blackburn's gaze shifted to Ann.

"If you are officers of the court, arrest that whore for stealing my gems!" His trembling finger pointed at Ann.

"Sir, there is no need to use foul language."

Josh spoke to Jackson, "This man is crazy, certifiable. The jewels he is talking about I found in that gap in the floor over there." Josh pointed to the damaged floor. "And then I gave them to the person-in-charge."

"All in this room have conspired against me. I want them arrested and taken to the gaol in Williamsburg." Blackburn was now seething with his rage.

"Sir, no one is conspiring against you," Jackson said in a soothing voice.

"Ask him what year it is," Josh piped in.

"We can handle this, sir." Jackson frowned at Josh as the mike clipped to his uniform shirt squawked. Jackson listened to the voice then depressed a button on the side of the mike and gave a code.

Em watched as Blackburn's rage lessened and his uneasiness increased as he stared at the electronic mike. "What trickery is this? How comes there to be a voice in yon box attached to thine apparel?" he said.

The mike squawked again, and Blackburn jumped and backed into Jarrod. Fear showed bright in his eyes. With no warning, Blackburn skirted around Jackson and sprinted for the outside door. Dewitt made a grab for him, but missed. He turned and chased after him. Jackson ran after Dewitt. Em and Josh followed Jackson out the door. When she arrived on the east wing porch, Em could see that Blackburn had turned and was running to the front of the villa, presumably to get his horse that had been dead for over two hundred years. Gripping the railing, she saw Blackburn come to a dead stop at the sight of the police vehicle.

Dewitt caught up to Blackburn, who was screeching with fear at the alien object in front of him. He grabbed Blackburn's arms and pulled them behind him as Jackson whipped out his handcuffs. He snapped on the cuffs then opened the back door of the vehicle as Dewitt tried to shove Blackburn through the door. Blackburn was having none of it, evidently deducing that he was being fed to the metal beast. Despite his hands being bound, Blackburn fought like a madman. The two officers finally manhandled him into the police cruiser, slamming the door shut. Officer Dewitt walked around to the driver's side as a crowd formed, questions buzzing. Blackburn continued to scream in terror as the car traveled around the circular drive.

"I hope the Petersburg Police Department issues earplugs," Josh quipped.

"Wow," Em said as Officer Jackson made his way back to the east wing porch. "I almost feel sorry for him."

"I don't," Josh said. "He would have hung Ezra if we had left him there."

Em sighed. "I miss him. I hope he had a good life."

"Me too," Josh said as Officer Jackson mounted the stairs.

It was another two hours before Em and Josh were allowed to leave. Because they were still minors, their parents were called to be present during their statement. While awaiting their parents, Josh and Em came up with a story to explain their filthy, torn costumes, and in Em's case, the burnt hem of her dress. They decided on a spontaneous climb down the bluff to the riverbank, a fall by Josh, and Em standing too close to one of the campfires. Both sets of parents showed up within a minute of each other.

Elizabeth took one look at Em's appearance and pulled her into her arms, crying softly. "My poor baby, what happened to you?" Em saw the concern on her dad's face over her mom's shoulder.

"I'm fine, really. I'm sorry about the dress, but I'll pay for it from my summer job at the recreation center."

"Oh, honey, don't worry about the dress right now. We'll pay Becky, and you can pay us back. Now tell us about this crazy person."

As Em started to explain, Josh's folks, David and Beth Winters, came through the door. Beth's dark layered tresses framed her worried face as she rushed to her son, exclaiming over his appearance. David, an older version of Josh, walked up to his son, gripped his shoulder, and asked if he was all right.

After the statements were given and paperwork signed, Officers Jackson and Dewitt shook hands with Josh, Em, and their parents, thanking them for their time. The teens walked with their parents to the Battersea parking lot. They waved good-bye as Josh stood next to his dad's car and reached into his left pocket for the keys. He pulled them out and stared at them for a minute.

"I forgot all about these keys while we were in the past. Isn't that funny?"

"They wouldn't have done us any good, anyway. They wouldn't have unlocked the room I was in."

Josh turned and stared at Em, the keys dangling from his fingers. "We did go back, didn't we? It wasn't some kind of dream."

Em could see the sudden doubt. The same *Am I insane* moments she had experienced when she came back the first time. Em gripped the hand holding the keys.

"Yes, Josh, it happened. I believe that God sent us back to 1770 because I begged for Martha's life." She paused. "And now we know why he kept us there. God wanted to give us the time to come up with a way to neutralize Blackburn so Ezra would be safe."

Josh gave Em a satisfied smile. "And we did."

EPILOGUE

One month later, on Josh's seventeenth birthday, Em stood proudly at her boyfriend's side as he was presented with a replica eighteenth-century sword by the Battersea Foundation. It was unseasonably hot and muggy, and Em's forehead shone with sweat. *Why, oh, why did the foundation decide to conduct the small ceremony at two in the afternoon?* Em and Josh stood on the front porch of the villa as the head of the foundation thanked him for finding the gems and handed him the sword.

Em looked out at the small group of people seated in white vinyl chairs as the photographer told Josh to hold up the sword and smile. Their parents and friends sat in the front row. The mothers were fanning themselves with the brochure they had been given on the Battersea Foundation. Josh's best friend, Tim, and Em's best friend, Megan, sat beside Caleb and Josh's fourteen-year-old twin sisters, Julia and Becca. Em smiled when she noticed Becca's blonde head turn and whisper to her brother. She caught Megan's eye, and she grinned and winked. Tim looked uncomfortable in his shirt and tie. He kept running a finger around the collar. Em turned her attention back to Josh as he shook hands with the head of the foundation and said thank you. Everyone clapped and rose from their seats.

"Em, is this not the coolest sword you have ever seen!" Josh turned the sword back and forth in his hands.

"It's beautiful. I'm glad Blackburn didn't have one of those stuck in his boot."

Josh laughed as he jumped down the three steps of the porch to show his dad the sword.

David gave Josh a one-armed hug. "Congratulations, son. That is a fine-looking sword. I'll take it back to the house with me, if you want me to."

After their friends and family had a chance to admire the sword, Josh and Em's parents said they would see them back at home and strolled around the circular dirt drive—with Caleb, Julia, and Becca—to the road and their vehicles. Josh, Em, and Megan were riding back in Tim's car.

Tim grabbed Josh's shoulder. "Okay, dude, let's see that hole in the floor where you found the treasure worth...what was it?"

"Almost one and a half million dollars," Megan said as she flipped her long french braid onto her shoulder.

Josh led the way along the side of the house to the east wing. The four teens climbed the stairs to the east wing porch and into the large room. Josh and Em stared at the spot where the gap in the floor had been. The broken board had been replaced, the newness of the replaced plank in stark contrast to the darkness of its two-hundred-and-thirty-year-old brothers.

"Well, so much for seeing the hole," Tim said as he yanked at his collar. "This tie has got to go."

He reached up and loosened the burgundy tie enough to slip it over his head and then unbuttoned the top button of his oxford shirt. He started to cram it into the pocket of his navy blue slacks and stopped. He switched the tie to his left hand and pulled a newspaper clipping from his pocket.

"Oh, yeah, I brought this for you to read. Josh, do you remember me telling you about our family time capsule? The one my great, great…I don't know how many *great*s grandfather locked up in a big metal box in 1900."

"Yeah?" Josh said.

"Well, we opened it last week, and you've been so busy that this is the first chance I've had to tell you about it. There was some cool stuff in there along with this really, really old letter dated 1824. And there was this really weird request at the top of the letter. My many *great*s-granddaddy that wrote the letter asked that it be published in all the newspapers in the vicinity of Petersburg. It was in the *Progress Index* this morning."

Josh's face still wore a quizzical expression. "But why do you want me to read it?"

"Because it's addressed to you," Tim said.

"What!"

"Just joking with you, my man. He was writing to someone named Josh." Tim handed the clipping to Josh.

"While you guys bond over the article, I'm going to show Megan the rest of the house," Em said.

She and Megan walked through the doorway and into the next room, while Tim wandered over to the window and looked over the grounds behind Battersea.

Josh looked down at the article. The first line made his heart start pounding in his chest.

> *To my fine friend Josh,*
>
> *I pray that this letter will find you after your travels back to your home. I am quite sure it was a destination that Master Blackburn would have wished to avoid.*

Josh smiled through the tears that were forming in his eyes.

> *You said that you wished you could know what happened to me once you had returned to your home, and I said I would*

find a way. I pray that I have succeeded. Upon leaving Master Banister's property on the mare you left for me, I decided to seek out Homer and convince him to accompany me on my travels. After much persuasion, he agreed. Hattie provided us with provisions, and we began our trek. It was arduous. Our journey was spent hiding from other travelers on the road. Many times we traveled through great forests with strange foliage. It was two months reaching our goal of Boston to the north. After many queries, I located my brother. Obadiah welcomed us with open arms. He concealed us in his home until the proper paperwork could be forged by a group of ardent abolitionists who do such for the runaways. My brother was quite well-to-do and owned a printing press. It was obvious to me from the first moment that my brother favored the British. I worked with Homer at my brother's establishment biding my time. Three years passed, and then one day that fine gentleman, Paul Revere, came through the door ordering advertisements for his silver working. As I was alone I took the opportunity to inform him that I wished to become a Son of Liberty. I was invited to one of their clandestine meetings, and so began my act of rebellion. I soon left my brother's establishment and home after a heated disagreement and obtained employment at the printing press of a fellow sympathizer of the rebel cause. As you have surmised, I survived the war and married soon after to a woman of great virtue and honesty. We had four sons— Joshua, Moses, Abraham, and Freedom. The gentleman whose employ I enjoyed allowed me to purchase his business upon his retirement. I renamed it the Lincoln Press after my surname.

Josh grinned, through the wetness, remembering their conversation on surnames.

I have reached my seventieth year and still feel as spry as the teen you remember me to be. My family is preparing for the move of our printing business to Petersburg. Word has reached us that many freed Negroes reside on Pocahontas Island and there is no newsletter for my Negro brethren. Colonel Banister has been dead many a year, and I wish to spend the last years of my life in the sweet south of my youth. Though I have lived most of my years in Boston, I have never had a fondness for its frigid weather. My sons and grandsons know of our secret, Josh, and will plan accordingly to ensure that this letter reaches you upon your return. You have had my undying gratitude these many years. I owe my blessed life to you and Miss Emily. I have never forgotten your last words to me. Now I shall pass them back to you. I love you, my fine friend.

—Ezra

Josh wept unashamedly as he dropped to the wooden floor overcome with emotion. Tim turned from the window at the sound of Josh crying and froze in shock and concern. He had never seen Josh cry and had no idea what had caused this emotional outburst. He walked over to his friend.

"What's wrong, Josh?" Tim crammed his hands in his pockets, unsure what to do.

The newspaper article shook in Josh's hands. "He did it. He did exactly what he said he would do. And he lived to at least seventy."

Still confused as to why Josh was so emotional over the article, Tim stated, "Actually Great-granddaddy Ezra lived to be ninety-eight years old."

Josh looked up at Tim as Ezra's face came to mind. For a second it seemed like Ezra's face superimposed on Tim's. Josh gasped in amazement. They both had a similar broad forehead and sharp nose. But it was the eyes that caused the pieces to fall in place because the shape was exactly the same for both teens. *Lincoln was Tim's last name!* And then. *The dream!* He now remembered that Tim had been bouncing a basketball and then stopped and told him to help his great-granddaddy or he would not be born. Josh jumped to his feet and shouted, "You were born! This is totally fantastic!" Josh raised his hands toward heaven. "Thank you, Jesus!"

Em and Megan rushed back into the room. Tim stood stunned in the middle of the room. Josh was shouting to the ceiling, his hands in the air and the fingers of his right hand gripping the newspaper article.

"Josh, have you lost your mind! People are wandering through the house. You sound like a madman."

"Em, he's alive! Or he was alive!" Josh, whooping with joy, rushed to her, picked her up, and twirled her around.

"Josh, put me down. Who's alive?" Em pushed on Josh's broad chest.

Josh set her on the floor. "Ezra! It's Ezra! Read this." Josh shoved the letter at her.

As Em scanned the letter, Josh strode over to Tim, who backed away warily until his back was up against the rear wall. Tears welled up in Josh's eyes again. "You look like him you know. Your great-greats-granddaddy, Ezra. I loved him like a brother."

Em whispered, "Ezra. It's from Ezra. How is this possible?" Em started weeping and laughing at the same time.

Josh turned and Em ran into his arms. Both started talking at once.

"Ezra!"

"I know."

"Can you believe it!"

Megan shouted to be heard over their celebration, "What is going on! You'd think it was the Second Coming or something."

Josh and Em looked at Megan and then looked at each other and grinned.

Josh said, "Em and I have a story to tell the both of you. But not here where we can be overheard."

"What story?" Tim asked warily.

"Well, the story about this letter, you see it was written to me."

The four teens stood under the huge oak that stood to the left of the villa. The same tree that Tim's many-greats-granddaddy, Ezra, had almost been hung on. Josh and Em had finished talking and waited for Megan or Tim to speak.

Josh fidgeted impatiently from one foot to the other. "Well?"

Tim's voice was raw with emotion when he finally spoke, "Normally, no way would I believe that God sent you back in time to 1770. I would figure my best friend has lost his mind, but..." Tim paused and put his hand in his left pocket and removed something from it. "This proves you're telling the truth." In his trembling hand was Josh's cell phone with the embedded musket ball. Both Josh and Em stood stunned and speechless. Unbelievably, it looked exactly the same as it had when Josh had seen it last on the ledge.

"This was in the time capsule."

"How did it..." Em said.

"I know," Josh interrupted. "Ezra must have put my cell phone in his pocket after he showed it to me on the ledge."

"No one in my family could figure out how this got into the time capsule. You can tell it's a cell phone. My dad wanted to know who jimmied the lock and put it there as a joke. Everyone swore they didn't touch the box. I asked if I could have it."

Megan spoke for the first time, "You're not kidding, all this is true?"

"Scout's honor," Em said as she held up the first two fingers of her right hand.

"Well, I think it's awesome! High five, Em." Megan held up her right hand and grinned. Em slapped her hand, and both girls dissolved into giggles.

Tim held the cell phone out to Josh. "I guess this is yours."

"No, Tim, you keep it. Ezra kept it in remembrance of our friendship, and he would want you to have it." Josh looked up. "Do you think he knows about us being best friends?"

Tears were forming in Tim's eyes as he looked up at the thick branch above his head. "Josh, you saved my greats-granddaddy Ezra from being hung on this tree."

"With a lot of help from Em and Ezra."

"And you brought Blackburn back here. Where is he now?"

"Locked up at Eastern State deciding what color of Jell-O he wants for dessert. That is if he is capable of making decisions."

Tim wiped a sleeve across his eyes. "Good." He reached his arms around Josh's back and hugged him until Josh thought his ribs would crack.

When Josh and Tim broke apart, everyone was wiping their eyes.

Em spoke into the sudden silence, "Hey, last time I came back from the past, I got to celebrate with ice cream. What do you say? Want to make it a tradition?"

"What?" Tim and Megan stared at Em. "Last time?"

Em laughed. "I'll tell you all about it over my cone of strawberry cheesecake."

"Oh no, you won't, Emily Grace, you tell me right now," Megan said.

"Okay." Em laughed as she draped an arm across her friend's shoulder. Josh did the same to Tim as the four teens walked out from under the shade of the oak tree and into the sun.